QUADRILLE

For Veronica

One

Augusta Fairfax sat bolt upright in her chair, doing nothing. In past years she would have been working at her tapestry, even though it frequently bored her, but the arthritis in her hands and her failing sight had put paid to that of late and there was nothing else she could think of to take its place. Miss Snettisham, her paid companion, sat in her less comfortable chair and at a suitable distance, working quietly on her embroidery. Other than the ticking of the ornate French ormolu clock on the mantelpiece, there was no sound to disturb the tranquillity, until Lady Fairfax's butler entered the drawing room, soundless as a cat, and bowed.

'Lord Nicholas is here to see you, milady.'

'Is he intoxicated, Mason?'

'No, milady. Not so far as I could ascertain.'

'Very well, you may admit him.'

She glanced at her companion who was surreptitiously patting her cap and rearranging her shawl. 'You needn't bother primping, Snettisham. You know he won't give a fig. Won't even notice, you.'

Miss Snettisham flushed and bent over her work again, but she raised her eyes timidly as firm footsteps sounded outside the door and Lord Nicholas Strickland strode in. Oh, what a handsome young gentleman he was! In all her days, which were more than she cared to remember, she had never seen the equal of him. So tall, such broad shoulders, such thick, dark locks, such fine features and such elegant dress and manners. And Lady Fairfax was quite mistaken for he often took pains to notice her. Indeed, after he had greeted his aunt with the most graceful of bows and a kiss on her cheek, he bowed again her direction and smiled at her too.

'Miss Snettisham, delighted to see you. How very fetching you look today.'

Her heart went pit-a-pat and the flush deepened. She stabbed wildly at her embroidery and pricked her finger.

'Don't tease her, Nicholas,' Lady Fairfax said sharply. 'You know very well that she does not.'

'On the contrary, Aunt Augusta, Miss Snettisham always looks most charming to me. As for yourself, I don't know when I have seen you look younger.'

'Flattery will get you nowhere. If you've come to ask for another loan, you're wasting your time. I'm not paying off your gambling debts again.'

Her nephew looked pained. 'How could you think that, my dear aunt.'

'Very easily. I've saved your bacon half a dozen times or more and I meant what I said on the last occasion. No more loans. It's time you stopped your wild ways, Nicholas. You'll be five-and-twenty next birthday. Time you were settling down. Choosing a wife. Behaving sensibly – like your elder brother. You should try to be more like him.'

'You know very well that I could never behave in the least like Edwin, Aunt. And if I did, that I'd bore you to death. Admit it.'

'I'll admit nothing of the kind. If you don't mend your ways, I shall disinherit you. I'm not having Maplethorpe being sold to pay your debts the minute I've left this world.'

'I promise you it will not be. You know perfectly how much I adore the old place. I love it as well as I love you, my dear and revered aunt.'

Lady Fairfax's stern and aristocratic features softened as she looked at her favourite nephew. He was standing before the fireplace, one highly polished boot propped on the brass fender, one arm resting along the marble mantelshelf, smiling fondly at her. Since a small child he had been a constant visitor to Maplethorpe, after the early death of his mother, her much younger sister. He was the son she had never had and, though she would never have let him see it, the joy of her life. He had grown from a reckless and charming boy into an even more reckless and charming young man. When he was twenty-one she had made him her heir. It was some compensation to him, she hoped, for being the younger son who would inherit neither the earldom that had gone to his elder brother, Edwin, on the death of their father, nor the family house and estates, and he had spoken nothing less than the truth, she knew, when he had said how much he loved Maplethorpe. He had spent a good part of his childhood here, preferring it to his own motherless home and the company of his worthy, but in Augusta Fairfax's private view, dull father and the even duller, Edwin. Secretly, she considered that Nicholas took after herself – that he had inherited her own zest for life, her own impatience with the mealy-mouthed, her own unbridled mettle – and for that reason she had repeatedly forgiven him his bad behaviour. She had overlooked the gambling, the racing, the drinking, the disgraceful extravagance, the loose women ... until now. Her patience had finally run out. Lady Fairfax drew herself up even straighter in her chair, one arthritic, beringed hand gripping the knob of her cane. She rapped it on the floor.

'I mean it, Nicholas. I have been thinking and I have reached a decision.'

'What decision, Aunt?' He was still smiling at her but this time she was immune.

'I have decided that the only way to change you is for you to marry.'

He looked astonished. *'Marry?* I assure you I have no intention of doing so at the present. Life is far too agreeable. Why should I wish to do anything so dreary?'

'Because I insist on it. Unless you agree to marry some suitable girl by the time you reach five-and-twenty then I shall have no choice but to disinherit you.'

He laughed easily. 'And have you any one in mind, dear aunt?

'As a matter of fact, I have. The perfect wife for you.'

His eyebrows rose. 'May I ask her name?'

'Charlotte Craven. The daughter of my old friend, Lady Craven. You will recall that they came occasionally to Maplethorpe in the past to visit us. I had not seen Charlotte for some while until recently and I decided then and there that she is exactly right for you.'

'Little Lottie! Don't be absurd, Aunt Augusta. She's still in the schoolroom.'

'Charlotte is eighteen and coming out this Season. No fortune to speak of but excellent breeding. Impeccable. I insist on that. Her mother was a Mildmay, you know.'

'Good God, is Lottie that old now? She was just a child when last I saw her. A funny little thing ... I remember her sitting like a mouse in the corner, scarcely uttering a word.'

'Naturally she didn't. Children should be seen, not heard. She has been extremely well brought up and will make you an excellent wife.'

He said, amused. 'I told you, Aunt, I have not the smallest intention of marrying anybody at the moment. Not for years and maybe never. I find the whole notion far too irksome. And, besides, I have yet to meet any marriageable woman that I cared for nearly enough.'

'Plenty of the other kind, though – from the stories I've heard,' Lady Fairfax said tartly. 'Some actress appears to be your latest paramour.'

'Tut, tut, Aunt. You're making Miss Snettisham blush.'

'She is not listening to things that do not concern her, are you, Snettisham.?'

'Oh, indeed, no. Lady Fairfax.'

'Except for Captain Young, you keep the most disreputable company, Nicholas, and it simply will not do. I will not endure the thought of such people polluting Maplethorpe one day. Sir George would turn in his grave, and so shall I. A suitable wife will see to it that such a thing never comes to pass. So, you may stop smiling now. I hope I have made myself clear? Either you marry Charlotte Craven before you become twenty-five or you will no longer be my heir. I shall leave this house and my entire estate to Edwin instead.'

'To Edwin! To *Edwin*! This whole thing

must be some strange joke on your part, Aunt. You know you could never support the idea of Edwin having your beloved Maplethorpe. Just imagine what he and his appalling wife might do to it.'

'I assure you that I should infinitely prefer that arrangement to entrusting it to your care, Nicholas. Edwin, at least, will ensure that it will remain safely within the family for generations to come and not be lost in some gaming saloon. And he has a legitimate son and heir.'

'Do you imagine that I am incapable of producing one?'

'I have no doubt that you are excessively capable – is something the matter with you, Snettisham?'

'Oh, no, my lady.'

'You sounded as though you were choking. I should be obliged if you would remain silent. I used the word *legitimate*, Nicholas, and for that you must be wed. Cockspur, the lawyer, is calling on me tomorrow morning and he will draw up the necessary papers ready for me to sign. The terms will be very clear. Charlotte Craven, or some other equally suitable bride of my choice, or nothing.'

His brow had darkened now, just as when he was a small boy, thwarted in some way. 'Come now, Aunt, you cannot mean this.'

'I most certainly do. It is high time you came to your senses, Nicholas.'

'But Edwin! And that spoiled, whining brat of his! It would be a monstrous...'

'The remedy lies in your own hands.'

He gestured vaguely. 'I'll think about it.'

'I suggest you do. I suggest you think very hard. And I also suggest you call on Lady Craven as soon as possible. She has already gone to town and taken a house in Mayfair for the Season. I intend spending part of the summer in London myself so I shall be able to follow your progress with the keenest interest. If you exert yourself sufficiently you may be able to persuade Charlotte to accept you before the end of the Season.'

'*Persuade* her, Aunt Augusta? I should have no difficulty whatever in doing that – should I so choose.'

Lady Fairfax smiled grimly. 'Not every girl is foolish enough to swoon at your feet, Nicholas. And I warn you, she has grown into an uncommonly sensible young wo-man.'

Two

'The plain fact of the matter, Lottie, is that neither you nor I have any likely expectation of finding a husband during the Season. You are too tall and I am too fat.' Miss Amelia Beauclerc spoke in dismal tones.

Charlotte Craven laughed. 'Don't sound so downhearted, Amelia. There is nothing so very dreadful about not having a husband. I came to that conclusion some time ago, having observed a number of the species. If necessary, we shall do quite nicely without them.'

'It's all very well for you to say that, but you are in far better circumstances than I.'

'Surely not. I have no fortune to inherit, like you. It is all entailed with Jack.'

'Oh, I know that. It's so *unfair* the way brothers must inherit everything, even though he is much the younger. But I am not speaking of any fortune. I meant that you are

16

quite content at home and your mama and papa are delightful and congenial people, whereas *mine* are both a great trial to me. Papa is invariably vile-tempered and Mama is constantly criticizing me and despairing aloud to all and sundry of ever getting me off her hands. I fear I am a sad disappointment to them in all respects. If it were not for my fortune, Mama says there would be no hope at all for me. And she is determined that it shall be a gentleman with a title. Nothing less than a baron will do, and preferably an earl. She is not so fanciful as to entertain a marquis or duke. But, I know I shall heartily dislike whomsoever she approves.'

'Then do not marry him.'

'You do not understand how hard it is to refuse anything of Mama, and Papa will not care so long as he is left in peace. I did not want to come to town at all but Mama insisted.'

'And I only did so to please my mama, too. I should far rather have remained in the country.'

Miss Beauclerc sighed. 'Well, there we are, Lottie. Both of us dreading the ordeal of a London Season. What is to be done?'

'Nothing but endure it. It may not be so

bad as we fear.'

'But look at me.'

'I am doing so.'

'How will any gentleman in his senses want to dance with anybody as fat as I? I shall be a wallflower at every ball.'

'You are *not* fat, Amelia. Just a little on the plump side and I think it suits you very well. To be truthful I cannot imagine you any other way. I am far less likely to be asked to dance for I will tower over most partners. It is *I* that will be the wallflower.'

'But you are not too tall, Lottie, merely taller than is usual for a girl. It suits you, too, and neither can I imagine *you* any other way.'

Charlotte laughed. 'We are a great comfort to each other, are we not?' She moved to the window and looked out on to the leafy square at two fashionable gentlemen passing. 'Come and see these two peacocks strolling by, Amelia. If they are a sample of what we will encounter then I, for one, will be very thankful if we are *not* asked to dance.'

Her friend peered past her. 'However long do you imagine it must take to achieve such perfection?'

'All morning, I dare say. Look, they hardly

dare set foot on the pavement lest a speck of dust mar the mirror shine of their boots.'

Miss Beauclerc giggled. 'Or move their heads for fear of disturbing their cravats. Oh, Lottie, if they are all like that then we need not worry what they think of *our* appearance for they will be far too occupied with their own'.

'More brandy, Clive?'

'Thank you, no, Nicholas. I think I've had enough.'

'I can tell by your face that you think I have, too. Censure is written all over it. If you were my Aunt Augusta you would be lecturing me on the evils of drink. Thank God you are not.' Lord Nicholas Strickland flung himself into a chair and tossed back a quarter of his newly filled glass. 'And, by God, I need this. Do you know what she is intending? Can you *imagine*?'

Captain Young smiled. 'Clearly something that you do not care for – that much is perfectly obvious.'

'She has gone too far, Clive. It is beyond all reason.'

'*What* is?'

'Unless I marry within the year, Aunt

Augusta is threatening to disinherit me and leave Maplethorpe to my brother Edwin.'

'That is certainly unfortunate, I agree. I take it that you have no one in mind that you would wish to marry.'

'You know very well that there isn't. Marriage is the very last thing in, or on, my mind. But that's not the worst of it. She has even stipulated *whom* I am to marry.'

'Anyone of your acquaintance?'

'Dammit, you seem to find this amusing, Clive. It's far from a joke, I assure you. Aunt Augusta is in deadly earnest. I am to marry Miss Charlotte Craven before the year is out or she will remake her will. Or, failing Miss Craven, another of her choice. She has conceived the ludicrous notion that such an alliance will ensure my good behaviour. The very reverse is more likely, if she did but know it.'

'I don't believe I've had the pleasure of meeting Miss Craven.'

'She's only just out this Season. A mere child. I've known Lottie since she was in the nursery – her mama and Aunt Augusta are bosom friends – though I haven't actually set eyes on her these past ten years.'

'What is she like?'

'A little mouse, as I recall. No looks to speak of. Nothing to recommend her, except that she didn't talk much – which, of course, might be considered by some to be a positive attribute in a woman. But can you picture me yoked to such a creature, Clive? I should be bored to death within a week. What is to be done?'

'If your aunt is as much in earnest as you say, then you are confronting a simple choice, my dear friend. Either you are bored to death, or you lose your inheritance and Maplethorpe.'

'I could support the loss of the inheritance, though I admit it would be excessively in-convenient, but to lose Maplethorpe would be unbearable. I love the damn place.'

'I know you do. Then there is nothing for it but to pay your addresses to Miss Craven and hope that she finds you more congenial than you her.'

'What are you saying, Clive? Why should she not? Women usually do.'

'In my limited experience, women cannot be relied on to do what is expected of them. She might not care for you, Nicholas. She might even turn you down.'

'Turn me down! Don't be ridiculous. She

is a little mouse – I told you. It will be a simple matter to charm her into falling into my arms. God knows, I've had enough practice. Pour me some more brandy, Clive, there's a good fellow.'

'What is your campaign to be, then?'

'Campaign? You are ever the soldier, Clive.' Lord Nicholas swilled the brandy round in his glass. 'First, we call on Lady Craven.'

'We?'

'The mamas of young girls tend to be somewhat wary of me. They are suspicious of my intentions. You will lend a reassuring air of honourable sincerity to the occasion.'

Three

Sophia Craven finished reading the letter from her old friend and laid it down beside her. The contents had given her much food for thought. On the one hand, Augusta's proposal that a match should be contrived between Charlotte and her heir, Lord Nicholas Strickland, appeared satisfactory, on the other she was afraid that, whilst it would secure her daughter's position and comfort, it might fail to secure her happiness. Rumours of Lord Nicholas's wild behaviour had frequently reached her ears and whenever she had encountered him over the years she had always privately considered him as unreliable as he was charming and handsome. There was only Augusta's word for the possibility that there was enough good in her nephew to justify entrusting her only daughter to him. *For all his recklessness, prodigality and unfortunate liaisons*, her friend had written,

I have always known there to be a far deeper and more worthy side to Nicholas. He is capable of great kindness and sincere affection and I firmly believe him to be capable of being an ideal husband and father, if only he can be persuaded to become one. As it happens, I have the means of persuasion and in your dear Charlotte, I am convinced, we have the perfect wife.

That Charlotte would make a perfect wife, was certainly true, Lady Craven considered. What was far less certain was that Lord Nicholas would make a perfect husband. And what was the means of persuasion referred to so casually? It would need to be investigated for Augusta was a stranger to scruple. And if her nephew needed persuasion then he must surely have displayed some reluctance. A reluctant husband was not likely to make a good one.

While she was lost in these anxious thoughts, Lady Craven's butler entered the room. 'Lord Nicholas Strickland and Captain Young present their compliments, milady, and beg leave to pay their respects.'

Speak of the devil, Sophia said to herself. Well, at least I shall have the opportunity of studying him at close hand. 'You may show them in, Clutterbuck.' She glanced at herself in the looking-glass over the mantel and made a minute adjustment to her lace cap. As she turned back, the two gentlemen entered the room. Oh, dear, memory had not deceived her. Lord Nicholas was as heart-stoppingly handsome as she had feared. His dark hair was artfully cut to give the very latest windswept look, and he was attired in a blue coat and doeskin breeches of the finest quality and tailoring. His cravat – its knot and starched white points so elaborately and elegantly arranged – had surely taken hours to achieve. He bowed low over her hand, greeted her most charmingly and gave her a smile that quite discomposed her. If she were twenty – no perhaps thirty – years younger she would have been hard put to resist him. His companion, more soberly clad in military uniform, was of most pleasant appearance and equally well-mannered.

'May I present a friend of mind, Captain Young. I believe you have not previously made his acquaintance?'

She received another bow, simpler in its

execution, and another smile, less dazzling, but very sincere. 'No, indeed. I am delighted to meet you, Captain Young. And to see you again, Lord Nicholas. Pray be seated. You are in London for the Season, I take it?'

'Yes, indeed. How is Sir Thomas?'

'Well, I thank you. He remains in the country with our young son, Jack, for the time being. He does not care greatly for London.' In fact, he detested it as much as his daughter and had seized on any excuse to remain there.

'Aunt Augusta tells me that you have taken this house for the Season, Lady Craven.'

Sophia inclined her head. 'Charlotte is out this year, you know. You remember Charlotte?'

'Little Lottie?' he said easily. 'I can scarcely believe that she is already old enough. When I last set eyes on her she was still in the schoolroom.'

'You will find her quite grown.' Too much, Lady Craven might have added. Charlotte had grown far more than was desirable in a young woman – not outwards but upwards, like a bean stalk. She had overtaken both her mama and papa by the time she was fifteen and it was a mystery from whom she had inherited such a height. Since all the ancestors had been painted sitting down they would very likely never know. But the fact was that to be taller than a good many gentlemen was a great disadvantage. A gentleman did not wish to have to look up to his wife. Sophia Craven eyed Lord Nicholas speculatively. He was certainly a good four inches taller than Charlotte, which might be the only real, practical recommendation for the match.

'I trust I may have the great pleasure of seeing Charlotte before too long, Lady Craven, and of renewing her acquaintance. Is she at home?'

Smoothly said, she thought; he is honey-tongued indeed. I do wonder what persuasion Augusta has brought to bear on him for I do not believe he can have any interest in my daughter for her own sake. Charlotte is a country-loving girl, without guile or sophistication, and rather too intelligent, as well as too tall, for her own good. *His* tastes are surely very different – from all that I have heard.

'Unfortunately not. She has gone out walking in the park with her friend, Miss Beauclerc. They have taken Marmaduke for an airing.'

'Marmaduke?'

Lady Craven smiled. 'Her dog. She would not be separated from him and brought him to London with her.'

He smiled too and once again her heart fluttered. It was such a delightfully slow, conspiratorial sort of smile and his eyes danced with mischief, if not devilment. 'Will he be attending the balls?'

'If it were Charlotte's choice, I'm sure he should.'

Captain Young leaned forward. 'He must be a very fine animal, Lady Craven. What breed is he? A little spaniel?'

She laughed. 'Oh, no. Marmaduke is nothing so respectable. He is a mongrel of very uncertain parentage. My daughter came across him abandoned as a puppy and adopted him immediately. He grew a great deal and does not resemble any breed I have ever seen. He has repaid her with complete devotion. If anybody tried to harm her I am certain that he would tear them to pieces.' There was the sound of some commotion from the hallway and loud barking. 'If I am not mistaken, that is them returned from their walk now.'

She had scarcely finished speaking when the door burst open. A large black and brown dog leaped in, followed by a tall young woman, bonnet clutched by its ribbons in one hand, dog leash in the other, hair and dress dishevelled, and a much shorter, plump companion with fair curls and cheeks scarlet from heat and exertion.

Lady Craven rose to her feet. *'Charlotte! What can you be thinking of to allow Marmaduke in here? Remove him immediately.'*

Her daughter was laughing and trying to catch hold of the dog's collar as he bounded gaily round the room. 'I'm sorry, Mama, he ran away when I took off his lead. He knew you were in here and came to say hello.'

It was Lord Nicholas who, at great risk to his immaculate breeches, put out a hand and siezed hold of the creature.

'Down, you undisciplined animal! Sit! I say. *Sit!*'

Marmaduke sat.

'This,' said Lady Craven in the sudden calm that followed, 'is Lord Nicholas Strickland whom you will doubtless recall from some years ago, Charlotte. And his friend, Captain Young.'

Miss Craven looked up from the dog and

glanced from one to the other. 'Which is which, Mama?'

'The gentleman holding on to Marmaduke is Lord Nicholas,' her mother said drily. 'Captain Young is the other.'

She bobbed a curtsey to each. 'I'm afraid that I do not remember you, Lord Nicholas. And Captain Young, I do not believe that we have ever met. This is my dear friend, Miss Beauclerc.' More bows and curtseys were exchanged. Charlotte attached the leash to the dog's collar. 'Thank you for catching him, sir. He *is* rather undisciplined, I know, but I am trying hard to train him to behave better.' She tugged the unwilling animal in the direction of the door. 'Come, Marmaduke, we must take you away. You have caused a great disturbance *and* you have dirty paws. You are a bad dog. Pray excuse us.'

The two young ladies and the dog left the room with more tugs and laughter and a wild scrabbling of paws on the polished floor. The door shut behind them.

Lady Craven sat down again. Her daughter's failure to remember Lord Nicholas had diverted her exceedingly, though naturally she did not show it. He had looked positively thunderstruck. In fact, he had appeared taken aback by the whole episode. If he had entertained any serious intentions, she guessed that they were now abandoned. Well, she for one, could not be sorry – for Charlotte's sake.

Lord Nicholas had remained standing. 'If you will excuse us, Lady Craven, we must take our leave of you. Another engagement calls us.'

She inclined her head graciously. Oh, but he was handsome...

'Good God, Clive. I can only suppose that Aunt Augusta has taken leave of her senses.' Lord Nicholas slashed furiously at the air with his cane as the two gentlemen walked away down the Mayfair street. 'How in the world can she have seriously thought I could ever be induced to marry that *hoyden*.'

'I thought you said she was a mouse.'

'Did I? A giraffe more like. No wonder her mama said that she had grown.'

'As I recall, you also mentioned that she was very quiet and never uttered a word.'

'Don't mock me, Clive. I am not in the mood for it. I remember her as quite different.'

'She, on the other hand, did not seem to remember *you* at all.'

'It's more than ten years,' Lord Nicholas said curtly. 'She was very young. I dare say I have changed, too, though I hope for the better, not worse, like her.'

'You are very hard on her. In my opinion she was delightful.'

'Then *you* marry her.'

'I do not stand to lose Maplethorpe. Besides, I doubt Miss Craven would have me. Or even you. She struck me as a very spirited young lady who would know exactly what she wants and does not want. Neither of us. I thought Miss Beauclerc was very charming too.'

'I scarcely noticed her – except that she was too fat instead of too tall.'

'She was very pretty. Did you not admire her eyes and her complexion?'

'No, I did not, though I can tell that you did. I was so appalled by Lottie that it drove everything else from my mind. As for that animal – I have never seen a creature less disciplined. She hadn't the least idea how to manage him.'

'He certainly obeyed you, Nicholas. You are always good with dogs.'

'Dogs are of no use unless they are well trained. They are merely a pest to everyone.'

'Well, when you marry Miss Craven you will have to get rid of Marmaduke – or train him. Perhaps you could train them both together.'

'I warned you, Clive, that I'm not in the mood for any jokes. And I have absolutely no intention of marrying her. Aunt Augusta is in town. I shall call on her tomorrow and tell her so.'

'You have never mentioned Lord Nicholas before, Lottie.'

'That is because I haven't seen him for many years. His aunt and Mama are old friends and we used to call on them occasionally in the country. Sit *still*, Marmaduke!'

'And you did not remember him? He is so *very* good looking that I am sure I should have done.'

'Oh, yes, I remembered him, Amelia. Very well. I remembered him as a highly conceited, spoiled young man who never troubled to exchange a single word with me. That is why I chose not to remember him today. One glance at him and I could see he had not changed a wit. So, I pretended not to know him.'

'He was exceedingly put out, you know. He looked quite *shocked*.'

'Did he? I imagine he is not accustomed to being forgotten.'

'It is strange that he came calling like that.'

'I cannot imagine why he did.'

'You don't think he might have an – interest in you, Lottie?'

'In *me*? Good gracious no! What an absurd idea! I have no fortune or looks to tempt a gentleman of his kind. I suppose he called out of politeness to Mama.'

'That must account for it. I confess I found him rather frightening. So very ... *worldly*. I should not know how to converse with him at all.'

'Fortunately, you were not obliged to. And neither shall I be. You will see that he will barely acknowledge us, should our paths cross.'

'Captain Young was different, I thought, didn't you?'

'Oh yes. Quite different.'

'Very nice looking and *sincere*.'

'Yes, indeed. I cannot imagine why he is keeping company with somebody like Lord Nicholas.'

'He had a very nice smile.'

'Captain Young, you mean?' Charlotte glanced at her friend. 'I can tell that you were rather taken by him, Amelia.'

'Just a little.'

'Well, I am sure that you will meet him again. Do get *down*, Marmaduke. You are a very bad dog indeed.'

'Did you notice how he sat when Lord Nicholas told him to do so? I have never seen Marmaduke obey anybody like that.'

'It was chance, that is all. Sit, Marmaduke. *Sit!*'

Amelia sighed. 'He never does with you, Lottie.'

The house that Lady Fairfax had taken for the Season was pleasantly situated overlooking Hyde Park, a few streets away from Lady Craven. It had been built in 1771 and the first-floor drawing room, with its magnificently carved ceiling and tall windows, directly overlooked the street. Miss Snettisham had cunningly positioned her chair so that, while seemingly engaged in her embroidery, she could glance out from time to time and see what was happening in the world outside. Life in the country, as Lady

Fairfax's companion, tended to be rather uneventful – if not actually plain dull – and occasionally Miss Snettisham longed for her existence to take a more exciting turn. She was not at all certain what form this excitement might assume, or what she wished it to be exactly, but in looking out of the window she could at least observe life passing her by, as it were, and take note. She watched the fine London carriages bowling along with their fashionable occupants, an elegantly accoutred horseman or two riding towards the park, a street sweeper with his broom, a nurse out with two little girls – Miss Snettisham gazed wistfully after those, aware that she was never likely to experience the blessing of her own children. A faint snore came from the wing-back chair by the fireplace where her employer was sitting. Miss Snettisham finished off the last petal of a carmine-red rose, snipped the silk and selected a skein of pale green from her sewing basket to begin the stem. A series of staccato grunts from the wing-back chair alarmed her for a moment, but Lady Fairfax's eyes remained firmly closed leaving her free to continue to look out of the window, on and off, for quite some time. She had finished most of the rose stem when a further inspection of the street revealed a tall figure that she instantly recognized, striding towards the house. Miss Snettisham gave a faint 'oh' and clapped her hand to her mouth. Her employer's eyes flew open.

'What is it, Snettisham? What are you doing?'

'Nothing, Lady Fairfax.'

'I distinctly heard you do something.'

'Oh, no, Lady Fairfax.'

'Just because my eyes are closed for a few seconds, I am not turned stone deaf.' Her ladyship tugged her shawl up round her shoulders as the butler entered. 'Well, Mason, what is it?'

'Lord Nicholas wishes to see you, milady.'

'Sober, is he?'

'As a judge, milady.'

'There must be something wrong with the boy. Show him in then, Mason.'

Miss Snettisham bowed her head over her embroidery, her needle trembling a little in her fingers. When Lord Nicholas entered the drawing room she permitted herself an upward glance. As usual, his lordship was all consideration. As soon as he had greeted his aunt, he turned and bowed to her most gracefully and enquired solicitously after her health. Lady Fairfax snorted.

'Stop simpering, Snettisham. That's quite enough, Nicholas. You'll turn her head. What is it you want this time?'

He took up his customary stance in front of the fireplace, one foot on the fender. 'I called on Lady Craven yesterday.'

'Did you, indeed? And did you see Charlotte?'

'Unfortunately, yes. And I have come to tell you, my dear Aunt Augusta, that whether I lose Maplethorpe or no, I have no intention of marrying that giraffe of a girl. I refuse absolutely. She is without grace, charm, looks, or even manners.'

'Come, Nicholas, that is not so, and well you know it. Charlotte may not possess conventional beauty and she may be a trifle on the tall side, but she is certainly not without looks. As for her manners—'

'She denied even remembering me.'

'Aha ... no wonder you are so displeased. How clever of her.'

'Clever?'

'Well, of *course* she remembered you. Who would not? But I dare say the memory was less pleasant than you supposed so she pretended to have forgotten – simply to pique you.'

He stared at his aunt for a moment and then, quite suddenly, smiled his dazzling smile. Miss Snettisham, all eyes and ears while appearing engrossed in her embroidery, caught her breath at the very sight of it. 'You may be right, but, in any case, I still do not intend to marry her. You will have to pick someone else.'

'I have come to a similar conclusion myself, since I am not persuaded that Charlotte would ever accept you.'

'I assure you that she certainly would.'

'No intelligent girl would be certain to do so, Nicholas, which is why I have been considering alternative candidates – all of them gently bred and virtuous but none cursed with a superior intellect. Snettisham, where is that list I wrote? What have you done with it?'

'It is on the table beside you, Lady Fairfax.'

'Huh, so it is. Now, Nicholas, here are the names of four. Three of them are just out this Season.'

'And the fourth?'

'Lady Anne Chelveden.'

'Good God, you cannot mean it! She has

been out for a dozen years at least. She must be more than thirty years old.'

'Then she will be all the more grateful for a proposal of marriage – even from you.' Lady Fairfax brandished the list. 'Here you are. If Charlotte Craven refuses you, then you take your pick of one of 'em and settle down, or I leave everything to Edwin. My mind is quite made up.'

He tweaked it out of her hand and glanced down the names, frowning. 'Miss Beauclerc? I encountered her at Lady Craven's.'

'She is a friend of Charlotte's, I believe. An only child who will inherit a considerable fortune. That should tempt you, Nicholas.'

'There is not a name on this list which could do that, Aunt Augusta.'

She shrugged, meeting his look implacably. 'Then you must somehow induce Charlotte to accept you. Pull the bell for Mason, Snettisham. Lord Nicholas is leaving.'

Four

By eight o'clock of the evening, Mr Roland Beauclerc was in an exceedingly vile temper. His gout, ever a torment, was playing up and the heat of the ballroom caused him great discomfort. He sat slumped in a chair, perspiring freely, his high, starched collar chafing his neck raw and his shoes pinching his feet. He had been obliged to stand up to partner strange females no less than four times and he was damned if he was going to do so again. He mopped his brow with a silk kerchief and said as much to his wife who sat beside him, watching the dancers with an eagle eye.

'Very well,' she responded, without turning her head and fanning herself briskly. 'But if you are going to sit there like a lump of lard, then at least you can observe your daughter more closely. *I* have not taken my eyes off her all evening and that is as it should be. We do not wish some penniless fortune hunter making himself agreeable to her. You know how foolish Amelia can be.'

With ill grace, Mr Beauclerc bestirred himself and paid grudging attention to the rich and colourful scene before him. A cotillion was in progress, each group of eight dancers moving round and round in circles beneath the glittering glass chandeliers – fine silks and satins, sparkling jewels and nodding feathers swirling in an ever-changing sequence so that he began to feel quite dizzy. He shut his eyes and opened them again, searching the crowded floor for his daughter, and found her partnered by some young man he had never set eyes on before.

'Who the deuce is that?'

'You may well ask,' Dorothea Beauclerc said tartly. 'He introduced himself as Captain Young and he is very likely of no consequence whatever. I shall make enquiries. Fortunately, she is engaged to partner Lord Pomeroy for the next. It is lucky that I secured him for her at the outset. I hear that Pomeroy Hall is one of the finest homes in the country. He looks to be a most suitable match.'

'Looks a damn fool, if you ask me.'

'I did *not* ask you, Roland. And considering Amelia's unfortunate size and gauche ways, I was afraid that not a single soul would ask her to dance. Just look at the way she is capering about! She has learned nothing from that French dancing master we engaged. *Nothing.* I do not know what I have done to deserve such a clumsy child.'

When the cotillion ended the couple watched their offspring approaching, accompanied to her seat by the captain who then bowed and withdrew. Mrs Beauclerc noted her daughter's flushed countenance and shining eyes with suspicion. 'I trust you have not engaged to partner that young man again, Amelia.'

'He did request it, Mama...'

'Out of the question. Two dances would be quite improper. And until I have learned more about Captain Young, you will refrain from conversing further with him. One cannot be too careful.'

'Of what, Mama?'

'Do not be obtuse, Amelia. Of fortune-hunters, of course.'

Her daughter flushed still deeper. 'Captain Young is a very true and honourable gentleman, Mama.'

'How can you possibly conclude that? You are but eighteen years old and you know nothing of the world. You do not imagine that it is your grace or beauty that he admires, since you have neither? He is a nobody, I suspect.'

'He is a good friend of Lord Nicholas Strickland, at any rate.'

'*Lord Nicholas Strickland!*' Mrs Beauclerc held up her hands in horror. 'That settles the matter. No acquaintance of his could possibly be honourable. You will not speak to him again, Amelia.'

'But, Mama—'

'Silence! Here is Lord Pomeroy come to claim his dance.' Mrs Beauclerc observed the mincing approach of his lordship with approval. 'Try to say something felicitous for a change and not to dance like a goat.'

Miss Craven, who had been feeling the heat almost as much as Mr Beauclerc, went in search of fresh air. She discovered a small anteroom with a door opening on to a balcony and stepped outside into the blessed cool of the evening. She would not, she decided, ever grow to love London. It stifled her. It was not only the closeness of the rooms and the crush of people but the need to behave constantly with such wearing propriety. To curtsey here and curtsey there, to smile and keep smiling, to sit still for hours, to converse on trivial subjects of no interest whatsoever, and to do so with people who seemed of little interest either. She had been invited to stand up with three of the most prodigiously dull young gentlemen that she had ever encountered in her life – and each one several inches shorter than herself so that she had been obliged to stoop to hear what inanity they were uttering next. The unhappy prospect of similar occasions stretching ahead for weeks to come filled her with gloom. She leaned her arms on the balcony railing and sighed. A slight movement from the other end of the rail startled her and a voice spoke out of the darkness.

'You do not appear to be finding the evening particularly enjoyable, Miss Craven.' The speaker stepped closer to the glimmer of candlelight cast through the open door so that she could see his face.

'Nor you, Lord Nicholas. Or you would not be out here either.'

'I should not be here at all, were it not for my esteemed aunt, Lady Fairfax, who prevailed upon me. I have attended far too many similar balls and find them infinitely wearisome as a rule. Do you not agree?'

He sounded in his cups, she thought. She could certainly smell strong drink. 'Well, I cannot say it is the equal of hunting.'

'There is a certain similarity, none the less.'

She caught his allusion at once. 'You mean that in the Season a ball is merely a chase of another kind – for a husband?'

'Or a wife.'

'It is strange that you have not yet found one – if you have attended so many.'

He took out a snuff box and opened it, taking a pinch. 'Tell me, did you really not remember me at all? Or was that a pretence?'

'Do you find it so very difficult to believe that any woman could forget you?'

'In general, they do not. Let me see, ten years ago you were eight and I should have been nineteen. We saw each other on some occasions when you visited Maplethorpe with your mama. Am I not correct?'

'It may be so.'

'And yet you still do not recall me at all?'

'I can recall somebody. Perhaps that was you.'

'What did you remember about that

somebody?'

'That he was hateful. Conceited. Condescending. Quite obnoxious.'

The snuff box shut with a snap. 'If I appeared so, I assure you it was quite unintentional.'

'My impression was rather the reverse.'

'Then you were mistaken, let me assure you. As for my own recollections, I remember *you* as a quiet little mouse. You'll forgive me for saying that you have changed somewhat.'

'You are implying that I am no longer either little or quiet? Both are perfectly true, and, as you were in search of peace and solitude out here, I shall spare you the disturbance of my company.' She did not wait for his reply, returning to the ballroom immediately and finding even its glasshouse atmosphere vastly preferable to his company.

'It is entirely as I suspected.' Mrs Beauclerc deposited her bulk on the slender chair beside her spouse, jolting him awake.

'What is?'

'I have this instant enquired of Lady Savernake. She tells me that Captain Young is, indeed, of no consequence. He is the third son of an impoverished baronet. Of what use is that?'

Her husband grunted. The short, stolen nap had refreshed him somewhat but his gout was still painful and, if anything, the room had become hotter. He thought longingly of his deep, soft feather bed and oblivion. The suitability, or otherwise, of his daughter's dancing partners had ceased to be the upper consideration in his mind. He took out his watch and consulted it, with relief. 'High time we called for the carriage.'

Captain Young ran his friend to earth on the anteroom balcony. 'What are you doing out here, Nicholas?'

'Contemplating the bleakness of a future without either an inheritance or Maplethorpe.' His lordship took a swallow from a silver brandy flask. 'I have made the acquaintance of two of my prospective brides and they are both purgatory, Clive. I danced with each of them in turn and wished myself at the other ends of the earth rather than in their company. They were the most empty-headed, vapid creatures I have ever had the misfortune meet.'

'You told me that there were four names.'

'The third was Miss Beauclerc. Since I am well aware of your own admiration for that young lady, I have eliminated her from the list.'

'I am obliged to you for that consideration.'

'To speak the truth, Clive, it is more in consideration of myself. She is pretty enough, I agree, now that I have had the opportunity to examine her more closely, but she is not to my taste. I wish you well in your pursuit of her, though I fear you may have some difficulty impressing her mama with your suit. Mrs Beauclerc puts me in mind of a prize sow guarding its only piglet.'

The captain smiled. 'She was barely civil to me, it is true.'

'By now she will have discovered precisely who you are and exactly your prospects. Nothing less than a title and five thousand a year would satisfy her. Being an only child, Miss Beauclerc stands to inherit a considerable fortune, according to my aunt, and so the title will be of greater importance than the prospects. Unfortunately, unless your two elder brothers predecease you without issue, you are a trifle deficient in that respect. I fear that a mother of Mrs Beauclerc's narrow vision will not trouble to enquire further or she might also discover that you are an officer of one of our finest regiments and of unimpeachable character, as well as being decorated twice over for extreme gallantry on the battlefield.'

Captain Young groaned. 'I did not know that Miss Beauclerc will inherit a fortune. That is bad news indeed.'

'Most suitors would consider it excellent news, Clive. Myself included.' Lord Nicholas took another swig of brandy and stowed the flask away in his pocket.

'Not me,' Captain Young avowed. 'For a woman, a large inheritance must be a misfortune rather than a blessing. *She* can never be certain whether she is pursued for her inheritance or for herself. And any suitor will have difficulty in convincing her that it is only for herself.'

'I do not believe you would have any such difficulty – you are transparently a gentleman of honour, unlike myself. The difficulty will lie in storming the pigsty – if you will forgive the figure of speech. Mine is in the lack of any attraction whatever.'

'Was there not another name that Lady Fairfax put forward. A fourth?'

Lord Nicholas shuddered. 'Lady Anne is well past thirty and closely resembles a horse. The last time I encountered her I recall that she smelled like one too. I do not think that even my aunt considered her a serious prospect.'

Captain Young shook his head. 'Then you are in a fix, Nicholas. Maplethorpe means a great deal to you, does it not?'

'I have loved it since a child. I cannot bear to think of it in Edwin's hands. He and that dreary wife of his would ruin the place. She has no taste, no sense of antiquity or beauty, no discernment ... And their snivelling brat of a son and heir is unlikely to improve with age. It would be a disaster.'

'There still remains the possibility of Miss Craven to avert such an catastrophe.'

'The least of all evils that present themselves.' Lord Nicholas sighed. 'Well, once we are married there will be no necessity whatever for me to see much of her. The occasional encounter will suffice. That's some consolation.'

'You are so sure that she will have you?'

His lordship flicked open his snuff box with a thumbnail. 'My dear Clive, of course she will. In the end.'

Five

'I think I may call upon Lady Fairfax, Edwin.'

The earl, seated at table in the dining room of his London house and intent upon his boiled mutton, nodded absently. 'If you wish.'

The countess frowned. Of late her husband appeared far more interested in his food than in almost anything else. He was growing quite corpulent, she had noticed. 'It is some time since we did so,' she pointed out.

'Thought you didn't care for Aunt Augusta.'

'I find her somewhat outspoken, certainly – even a trifle uncivil – but she is your aunt, after all. Your flesh and blood.'

'True.'

'Who is growing old.'

'Very true.' The earl poked fussily at a piece

of fat. 'I suppose she cannot have long left in this world.'

'And then what is to happen to her fortune, which must be considerable? And to Maplethorpe?'

'All left to Nicholas. You know how she favours him. Always has. Never understood why.'

The countess drew herself up, purse-lipped. 'Your brother is a worthless profligate. It is monstrous that he should inherit a single penny. All he will do is gamble everything away or spend it on loose women – like that actress he has been in company with of late. A brazen *strumpet*. Now, if Lady Fairfax were to leave it all to *you*, Edwin, it could be spent wisely. We could make improvements to this house, as well as to Strickland Hall. You have all the expense of their upkeep to bear. Lady Fairfax should make *you* her heir. Besides, you are the elder nephew.'

'True.'

'I wish that you would not keep saying that, Edwin. Of course it is true.'

The earl examined another piece of mutton. 'I wasn't aware that you liked Maplethorpe, my dear.'

'I do not – at least, not in its present state. There are changes which would need to be made immediately. That old west wing should be pulled down, for instance. And I cannot abide the way the house *rambles* so untidily. But, with considerable alteration, it could be much improved. And besides, what has Nicholas done to deserve it? He is without principle or a shred of responsibility whereas you, Edwin, are the very soul of probity and trustworthiness. And what is more, you have a son and heir to continue the family line. I doubt your brother will ever be wed, unless it be to one of his dreadful paramours.'

The earl chewed on a mouthful thoughtfully. 'Aunt Augusta likes him.'

'Because he flatters her, that is why. He fools her with blandishments while he borrows money to pay for his gambling debts and loose living. And the older she grows the easier it will be. He is a disgrace to the Strickland name.' The countess rose purposefully from the table. 'I shall call on Lady Fairfax tomorrow morning.'

Miss Snettisham had started work on a new piece of embroidery. Instead of roses it was daisies and she welcomed the change. Roses were all very well but a great trouble to make look right, while daisies were simple. She was not a very gifted needlewoman, sadly, and her work did not always turn out as well as she had hoped at the beginning, but she persevered, for what else was there to do with the long hours in a day? She occasionally played a hand or two of bezique with her employer but her card-playing skill was equal to her embroidery and her ladyship frequently lost patience. Once she had sat down at the pianoforte to go through her small repertoire of pieces but halfway through her employer had put her hands over her ears and complained of a headache.

On this morning Lady Fairfax had not yet risen, due to a particularly painful attack of arthritis, and so Miss Snettisham was free to gaze out of the drawing-room window whenever she so chose. She had finished two daisies when a carriage drew up outside the front door but though she stood up to peer through the glass, she could not quite see who was inside.

After a few minutes Mason opened the door and announced the Countess of Strickland. Miss Snettisham, much flustered, rose to her feet, dropping her embroidery on the carpet.

'Oh ... pray excuse me...' She retrieved the tambour hurriedly and curtseyed. 'Her ladyship is indisposed ... I fear that you may be disappointed...'

The visitor regarded her frigidly. 'Mason informs me that Lady Fairfax is expected to descend shortly. I shall await her.' She sat down – by mischance in Lady Fairfax's particular chair – though Miss Snettisham, who had never met the countess – or any countess – before, did not like to say so. She resumed her embroidery, observing the visitor covertly between stitches – the humourless face, the unstylish mud-coloured gown, ill becoming either her ladyship's figure or her complexion, and the bonnet, its brim heavily adorned with limp orange and brown feathers that gave the unfortunate impression of a dead fox. Miss Snettisham recalled Lord Nicholas once referring to his sister-in-law as 'that depressing creature.' The mantel clock ticked on in the uneasy silence broken, at length, by the countess.

'I have no recollection of you from previous visits. There was some other person before.'

56

Miss Snettisham hastened to introduce herself. 'I have only been in Lady Fairfax's employ for three months.'

The countess stared for a moment before speaking again. 'Are you acquainted with Lord Nicholas Strickland?'

Miss Snettlesham blushed a little. 'Yes, indeed.'

'Does he call frequently on Lady Fairfax?'

'Oh, yes. Quite frequently.'

'And you are present on such occasions?'

'Usually. Though, of course, it is not my place to take part in any conversation.'

'But you listen to what is being said?'

Miss Snettisham blushed deeper. 'I cannot help *hearing*.' To her surprise Lady Strickland suddenly bestowed a gracious smile – as startling as a bright ray of sunlight on a grey winter's day.

'I confess that I have been much concerned about Lord Nicholas of late. I speak in the strictest confidence, of course. You will doubtless be aware that he leads a most dissolute existence. The earl and I had hoped that, with the passing of years, he would mend his ways but from all that I hear this is far from the case. Quite the contrary. It is a *great* anxiety to his brother and myself.' The countess, appearing much concerned, leaned forward confidingly. 'I am certain that Lady Fairfax cannot be unaware of this, however much Nicholas might try to conceal it from her.'

'No, indeed ... that is to say ... what I mean is that very little escapes the notice of her ladyship.'

'As I feared.' The dead fox rose and fell dramatically. 'Poor, foolish Nicholas.'

'To speak the truth,' Miss Snettisham avowed, 'I have also been quite anxious on his lordship's behalf, myself. There is the inheritance, you see ... Oh, dear, I should not even *mention* such a thing...'

'You may speak openly with me. I am well aware that my brother-in-law is Lady Fairfax's heir. What of it, Miss Snettleshun?'

The countess had mispronounced her name, but no matter. Miss Snettisham was flattered by the very close attention being paid to her – so rare an occurrence in her life. 'Well, her ladyship wishes his lordship to be married.'

'*Married?* To whom, pray?'

'To a Miss Charlotte Craven. Her ladyship considers that Miss Craven would be a good influence on Lord Nicholas.'

58

'Has Lady Fairfax told him so?'

'Oh, yes. In this very room, the other day.'

'I cannot imagine my brother-in-law willingly accepting such direction, or taking any bride likely to exert a good influence on him. He consorts only with women of the worst possible kind.'

Miss Snettisham blushed still deeper. 'Indeed, he was *not* in the least willing – that is until Lady Fairfax threatened to disinherit him if he did not marry Miss Craven.'

The countess's mouth opened, and then shut again with a snap. 'And what did he have to say to that?'

'At first he laughed. I do not think he believed that her ladyship truly meant what she said. And when he saw that she *was* perfectly serious he refused point-blank to entertain such a step. Then, later on, Lady Fairfax showed him a list of some other young ladies and said that if it was not to be Miss Craven then it must be one of them.'

The countess had leaned even further forward. She clearly valued what Miss Snettisham had to say; why, she was hanging upon her every word. 'And how did he answer?'

'He replied that not one of them could ever tempt him.'

'Did he, indeed? What then?'

'Well, after that her ladyship was very firm. "In that case," she told him, "you must marry Miss Charlotte Craven within the year or I shall leave all my fortune and Maplethorpe to—"' Miss Snettisham clapped her hand over her mouth in distress. 'Oh dear, oh dear, I did not mean to utter a word ... how very indiscreet of me. Whatever will Lady Fairfax say? Oh dear, oh dear.'

The countess said quickly in soothing tones, 'I assure you that she will not hear of this from me. But I trust she is not proposing to name somebody outside the family as her new heir? Surely not?'

'Oh, no, your ladyship need not worry on that score. It is to be the elder brother of Lord Nicholas. The earl, your husband.'

As she spoke the words the sound reached their ears of Lady Fairfax's flailing descent from the upper floor. Miss Snettisham turned quite pale. 'I beg that you will not mention our little conversation, Lady Strickland.'

The countess gave a grim smile. 'So long as *you* do not, Miss Snettleham, I shall remain silent.'

'A most successful visit, Edwin.'

'How was Aunt Augusta?'

'Her customary uncivil self. I find her excessively trying but I concealed it well, I trust. Her bluntness is most offensive at times.'

'She's always been the same. Takes pleasure in it.'

'Be that as it may, *I* do not. But before she came downstairs I had a most *interesting* conversation with her new companion – a Miss Snettlesun, or some such peculiar name. A very unremarkable person. Scarcely noticeable at all. However, I had the foresight to question her about your brother.'

'Oh?'

'It seems that your aunt has at last lost all patience with his disgraceful behaviour. She has told him that unless he marries suitably within the year she will disinherit him entirely.'

'Good God!'

'Pray refrain from profanity, Edwin.'

'Can't imagine Nicholas meekly obliging.'

'He will have to, if he wishes to keep his inheritance. He is to marry a Miss Charlotte Craven or he will lose everything – including Maplethorpe.'

'Still can't see him doing it.'

'For once, you are right, Edwin. Miss Snettleton informed me that your brother refused point-blank. And, more to the point, when Lady Fairfax showed him a list of other possible brides that she had compiled, he would not consider any of them either. Not one. And the very *best* part is that your aunt is to will all her estate to you instead if he does not do as she says. We need not have concerned ourselves.'

The earl fingered his chins. 'Nicholas might change his mind, if it suits him. He could marry the girl – or any of 'em, if he's a mind to do so. They'd never refuse him. No woman ever does.'

'It will not happen.'

'Huh. Don't know how you can be so sure, Maria.'

'Because I shall make very certain that they know the reason. I shall begin with Miss Craven. She is the preferred choice of your aunt. If your brother changes his mind, it will be her that he will pursue.' The countess paused triumphantly at the doorway, about to leave the room. 'You may safely leave everything to me, Edwin. Maplethorpe will be ours.'

Six

Marmaduke being a dog in need of a great deal of exercise, Charlotte took to walking with him daily to Hyde Park. Her friend, Amelia Beauclerc, frequently accompanied her – when she could escape from her mama – and on a fine summer's morning they set forth from the house in Mayfair with Marmaduke dragging Charlotte along at the end of his leash.

'He behaves no better, does he?' Miss Beauclerc observed, seeing Charlotte's arms being almost pulled from their sockets. 'I thought he might have learned a little by now.'

'It is because he knows very well that we are going to the park. He hates being cooped up in the house. So do I.'

Amelia was less certain about her own feelings on that subject. Walking was all very well but she would have preferred to proceed more slowly, especially since the day was so hot and her lace parasol of little real use against the sun's glare. With Marmaduke setting the pace, they must always scamper along. Charlotte, of course, did not mind a jot but then her legs were a great deal longer. By the time they reached the gateway to the park Amelia was out of breath and perspiring. She fanned herself with one hand. 'I cannot go any further for the while, Charlotte. I must rest in the shade.'

'Very well, let us go over to the trees. I shall let Marmaduke off his leash so he may run about.'

It was pleasantly cool beneath the trees and Amelia furled her parasol and sank down on to the grass. 'I dare say I shall get stains on my gown and Mama will be angry, but I do not care.'

Charlotte was unleashing her pet who was in a frenzy of excitement. 'There you are, Marmaduke, off you go – but not too far, mind.' She sat down beside her friend. 'I am rather glad to rest too. He has so much energy. I don't know when he will ever outgrow it.'

'How old is he?'

'That's just the trouble, I have no idea.

When I found him wandering about on his own, he was much smaller, of course, but exactly how old he was then I couldn't say. You can see that he is still only a puppy.'

Amelia looked doubtfully at Marmaduke gambolling wildly about. 'Then he is the largest puppy that I have ever seen.' A group of military gentlemen riding by along Rotten Row caught her eye. One of them resembled Captain Young a little. She gave a deep sigh. 'Mama has said that I must never speak with Captain Young again, you know. She says he is a fortune-hunter but I cannot believe it. He seemed so *very* nice.'

'He certainly did not seem to me at all like a fortune-hunter.'

'Mama says that anyone who is a friend of Lord Nicholas Strickland cannot possibly be trustworthy. Do you think that is really so?'

'I believe there is a saying that one may judge a man by the company he keeps, but I do not know how true it is.'

Amelia gave another sigh. 'Well, I do not believe Captain Young to be a fortune hunter. I believe him to be good and true, in which case Lord Nicholas cannot be so bad as everybody believes. Can he?'

'He is likely much worse.'

'Well, when he spoke to me at the ball he was perfectly civil and not nearly so frightening as I had thought.'

'He spoke with you?'

'Oh, yes, did I not tell you? He engaged me in conversation early on in the evening and for quite some time until Mama came upon us. If he had not had such a wicked reputation, I dare say she might have been quite pleased for I know she wishes me to marry a title. That is why she favours Lord Pomeroy.' Miss Beauclerc made a very indelicate retching noise. 'He makes me feel quite sick with his prancing and primping. Do you know that he paints his face, like some old people do, and I cannot abide that in a gentleman.'

'Nor I.'

'And he is so doused in strong perfume I must hold my breath whenever he comes near. And yet Mama is forever remarking on what a fine gentleman he is. I do not think he is so at all. Captain Young is much finer. Oh, what am I to do, Lottie? I dare not disobey Mama and yet I should so much like to talk with Captain Young again and make his acquaintance further for I am quite sure that he is not hunting my fortune.'

'Perhaps the chance may come. Have a care though, Amelia, in case your mama is right about him.'

They sat for a while, cooling themselves in the shade, and watching the carriages drive by and the riders out along Rotten Row. A herd of deer grazed peacefully in the long grass nearby and, at a further distance, the waters of the Serpentine glittered in the sunshine. London was not so bad, Charlotte decided, though she would still have much preferred to be in the country. She was watching the deer when a cacophony of barking and yelling and neighing broke out and she turned her head to see Marmaduke dancing round the heels of a large grey horse on the Row, with its rider shouting furiously at the dog and thrashing at him with his crop. The horse was plunging about and lashing out and Marmaduke, who seemed to think it all a fine sport, was dodging both crop and hooves and barking delightedly.

'Oh, you stupid dog!' Charlotte leaped to her feet. 'Come here at once. *Come here, Marmaduke!*' The wretched animal took no notice of her at all but only barked the louder. Charlotte watched in horror. Either the rider would be thrown from his horse and be badly hurt or Marmaduke would be killed. She ran as fast as she could across the grass towards the Row and, in her headlong haste, tripped over a tussock and fell heavily to the ground. Amelia running after, but more slowly, came upon her friend wincing with pain from a twisted ankle. Charlotte struggled to her feet, tried a few steps and gave up.'

'It's no use, Amelia. I cannot use it for the moment. Will you see if you can go and call Marmaduke off.'

'I'll try, Lottie, but you know he will not take any notice of me.' She approached the chaotic scene fearfully. 'Marmaduke! Come here. Come here at *once*.' Of course he did no such thing and Amelia stood helplessly, not daring to go closer. Then somebody else called the dog's name loudly, and in a voice that brooked no argument. Marmaduke looked round and, at the sound of a second command, turned away from the horse and trotted obediently in the direction of the voice. Amelia stared in astonishment as he lolloped towards two gentlemen riders coming along the Row. Her astonishment turned to delight as she recognized one of them as Captain Young; the other, the owner of the voice, was Lord Nicholas Strickland. Heedless of decorum, she ran towards them, waving her parasol.

'Oh, Captain Young ... Lord Nicholas ... I am so very glad that you are here. I did not know what to do. We were trying to stop Marmaduke but poor Lottie fell and hurt her ankle...'

Both gentlemen had dismounted and Captain Young hastened to her side. 'Please do not alarm yourself, Miss Beauclerc. We shall look after Miss Craven, will we not, Nicholas?'

His lordship was already leading his horse over to where Charlotte was standing like a heron on one foot. Marmaduke trotted docilely after him.

'You have hurt your ankle, Miss Craven?'

'I fell and twisted it a little, that's all. It's nothing to make a fuss about.'

'I never fuss,' Lord Nicholas informed her. 'Can you walk on it at all?'

'Not very well.' She tried another step and winced again.

'In that case you had better ride home on my horse.'

'I should much rather not.'

'I dare say, but there seems to be little

alternative at present. I shall lead him so you need have no fear.'

'I am not afraid,' she said indignantly.

'Then take my arm. Lean your weight on it.'

She did as he ordered, though not as meekly as Marmaduke, and hobbled painfully to the horse's nearside. The animal – a fine black thoroughbred – stood perfectly still while Lord Nicholas put his hands about Charlotte's waist and lifted her up to sit sideways on the saddle. Her muslin skirts rose halfway up her calves, with petticoats and stockings in full view; Amelia hurried forward to arrange matters more modestly. 'Are you all right, Lottie?' she hissed, standing on tiptoe. 'Would you prefer to ride on Captain Young's horse?'

Charlotte whispered back. 'I cannot very well get down now, Amelia. Besides, what difference would that make?'

'But your reputation, Lottie ... Well, *his* reputation, is what I mean. You are up there for all London to see. Like – like a trophy! Whatever will your mama have to say?'

'I imagine that she will be pleased to have me safe home, not lying in Hyde Park.'

'Captain Young and I will walk very close

behind you all the way.'

'And what will *your* mama say, if *that* should come to her ears?'

They set off with Lord Nicholas leading his horse at the bit, Marmaduke following, and Captain Young and Amelia on foot behind them, the captain leading his bay. Charlotte was dismayed by her absurd situation. To have been forced into such unwelcome company was bad enough, but the awkward circumstances made it even worse. She could not easily sit sideways on an ordinary, gentleman's saddle and had to grip hard on to the pommel in order not to slide off. Lord Nicholas observed her predicament and, before she could argue the point, swung himself up into the saddle behind her to hold her steady. Two dowagers bowling by in an open carriage raised lorgnettes in shocked tandem.

'Oh dear, Lottie's mama will not approve of that at all.' Amelia told the captain anxiously.

'I think it is safer,' he replied. 'Lord Nicholas only wishes to see Miss Craven unharmed.'

She was partly reassured. 'Well, it is very kind of him to take the trouble. And you,

71

too, Captain Young. I do not know what I should have done otherwise. I could not have left Charlotte on her own there to go for help, and one does not like to approach total strangers. What good fortune it was that you should come along.'

'The fortune was mine, Miss Beauclerc,' he said candidly. 'I had been hoping that somehow I should be able to meet and talk with you again but I fear that your mother does not wish it.'

'To be truthful, she does not.' Amelia blushed with embarrassment. 'I cannot explain why.'

'I know why and I understand. It is only natural that she should wish the very best for you. Any mother would do so.'

'But I do not care in the least for the people *she* likes.'

'I am glad to hear you say so, but you may yet change your mind before the Season is out.'

'I shall *never* change my mind about Lord Pomeroy.'

He hesitated. 'Perhaps we may at least see each other at functions, even if we may not converse?'

'Oh, I do so hope we do,' she said earnestly

and she turned her head to give him a sweet and unaffected smile. Against all his honourable intentions, the captain's heart was completely and irretrievably lost.

They reached the Mayfair house and Lord Nicholas lifted Charlotte down from the horse's back. Lady Craven, who had seen the party's clattering arrival from the window, and her daughter borne on the horse's withers with his lordship's arm about her waist, hurried out, scandalized. 'Charlotte, what *can* you be thinking of, making such a spectacle of yourself! Lord Nicholas, I am appalled at your conduct. Such impropriety! I had thought better – even of you.'

Charlotte limped towards her. 'Please calm yourself. Mama. It was not improper, merely expedient. I twisted my ankle in the park and could not walk back. Lord Nicholas and Captain Young happened to be passing. It was all Marmaduke's fault.'

Lady Craven looked bewildered. 'Marmaduke's fault?

'He was chasing after a horse and rider. I ran to try and stop him and fell. That is all.'

'I might have known that wretched animal had done some mischief.' Marmaduke, skulking at Lord Nicholas's heels, lowered his ears and tail. 'I will not have him in this house any longer, Charlotte. He must be given away. He is *too much*.'

'If you wish, Lady Craven,' Lord Nicholas offered casually, 'I should be happy to remove the dog. I can promise to teach him his manners and return him to Miss Craven when he has learned how to behave.'

Her ladyship looked at him askance. 'I am not certain that you would be a good tutor in matters of behaviour, Lord Nicholas.'

'Where animals are concerned, you will find that I am.'

'Indeed, it was Lord Nicholas who stopped Marmaduke from baiting the horse,' Amelia declared. 'He had only to call him and he obeyed, whereas he takes no notice at all of Lottie or me.'

Lady Craven conceded. 'Then I shall be obliged to you, Lord Nicholas.'

'But *I* shall not, Mama,' Charlotte protested. 'Marmaduke is *my* dog and shall stay with me.'

'No, he will not,' her mother said with great firmness. 'Not until he has learned his manners. Nor shall we stand on the doorstep one minute longer, making a further spectacle for all in the neighbourhood to enjoy.

Gentlemen, I thank you for bringing my daughter safely home and I bid you good-day.'

Lord Nicholas and Captain Young mounted and rode off with Marmaduke loping along behind them.

The captain shook his head. 'Good God, Nicholas what in heaven's name made you take on this impossible mutt. What shall you do with him?'

'Teach him his manners, like I said.'

'A hard task, I think.'

'I have always found it simple enough. In general, dogs are anxious to learn. And consider the advantage, Clive. If I am to marry Miss Craven then Marmaduke will be ready trained.' Lord Nicholas smiled slowly. 'I may even let her keep him.'

Charlotte was reclining on the sofa in the drawing room, resting her ankle, when Lord Nicholas called at the house two days after the incident in the park. Her immediate inclination was not to receive him, but then she decided that this would be somewhat ungracious after his Good Samaritan act and, besides, she would be able to enquire after Marmaduke's well-being. 'You may show him in, Clutterbuck.'

He walked into the room and she could not help but admit to herself that he cut an exceedingly fine figure. His attire was entirely plain and unostentatious – the handsome effect resulting from perfection of cut and style and impeccable grooming. It appeared artless but she had a suspicion that considerable pains were taken to achieve it. He bowed and enquired very civilly after her mother's health and her own. Equally politely, she invited him to sit down.

'Mama is not at home, I fear. In fact, she has gone to call upon your aunt, Lady Fairfax.'

'It was *you* I came to see.'

'Oh? Is it about poor Marmaduke?'

'No, it is about your ankle. I wished to be quite sure that all was well.'

'It is much better, thank you. The doctor says that no bones are broken and it is nothing more than a sprain. I am to rest it for a few more days and then shall be able to walk about as normal.'

'That is very good news.'

She was puzzled by his apparently sincere concern; he surely could have no more interest in her welfare than mere politeness demanded. 'Please tell me, how is Marmaduke?'

'In fine spirits. He is outside, waiting by my carriage.'

'You are sure that he is happy?'

'Perfectly. He has been well fed and well treated and is learning rapidly.'

'You have not been unkind to him – beaten him?'

He smiled. 'I swear to you that I have never laid a hand on any animal. He is quite safe with me.'

'And you will return him soon?'

'As soon as he has acquired sufficient manners for your mama to tolerate him.'

'He *is* something of a trial, I admit. But he does have a very affectionate and loving nature, though his looks do not at first commend him.'

'Indeed they do not, but, like wine, he may improve with age. I judge him to be less than a year old and his parentage deerhound and sheepdog. Excellent breeds in themselves but an unfortunate mix. Still, he has had the good fortune to win your heart.'

He was looking at her as he spoke and she met his gaze uncertainly. The attention he was paying was very strange indeed and she wondered, as at the ball, if he was perhaps drunk, though he did not seem to be. He had never shown the least interest before. On the contrary. She could so clearly recall how on his visits with his aunt he used to ignore her and how, on one occasion, when prevailed upon to play a game of ludo with her he had done so with marked ill grace, not troubling to conceal his boredom. She had watched him secretly on all those visits and, early on, formed a very unfavourable opinion of his character. Her first encounter after the gap of years had not altered that opinion. Now, she was not quite so sure. She turned her head away towards the window and took refuge in small-talk. 'What a beautiful day! I can see how blue the sky is.'

'You would see it far better from outside,' he remarked easily. 'We could drive into the park in my carriage. There is nothing better for sprained limbs than taking the air.'

'Mama might not agree with you.'

'Surely she could have no objection? After all you would be sitting beside me this time in a perfectly acceptable manner.' She demurred, still uncertain of him, but it was hot and stuffy in the room and the cooling breeze wafting in from the half-open window was very tempting. 'And you will see Marmaduke,' he added. 'He will come with us.'

'In that case...'

Her bonnet, a light shawl and a parasol fetched, she was ready to set forth and once again leaned on his arm for the short walk required to the carriage. Marmaduke, seeing her, leaped forward in rapture and bounded around, barking, but on a sharp reprimand from Lord Nicholas checked himself and returned to his appointed place by the wheels. The carriage, she saw, was an exceedingly smart two-wheeled curricle attended by a liveried groom and harnessed to a pair of perfectly matched greys. Lord Nicholas helped her up on to the seat, having a great care for her injured ankle, and took his place beside her while the groom vaulted up at the back. He handled the horses as smoothly as she had expected and they made a fast pace towards the Park, bowling along with the big dog running easily behind them. She remarked upon the fineness of the equipage.

'I won it at cards,' he told her, with a dry smile. 'A lucky hand, another's misfortune and the horses and carriage were all mine.'

'Do you often win such things?'

'Occasionally. I once won a very beautiful black panther with a collar of emeralds. I gave the panther to the zoo and kept the emeralds.'

She remembered his reputation, the whispers she had heard. 'You gamble a great deal, do you not?'

'Yes,' he agreed. 'It's a bad habit of mine. My aunt is always trying to cure me of it. As well as of other bad habits. She despairs of me.'

She did not enquire further about the other habits; she had heard whispers about them, too. 'Perhaps, like Marmaduke, you will improve with age.'

He laughed. 'Perhaps.'

'You are very fond of your aunt, Lady Fairfax, I believe.'

'Very. She has been good to me over the years. Indulged me far more than she ought, if the truth be known.'

Remembering his sulks and wilfulness in the distant past, she agreed wholeheartedly, though it was surprising to hear him admit it. 'You have an elder brother, is that not so?'

'Edwin. Did you never meet him? No, I suppose you would not. He rarely came to

Maplethorpe. He and his wife are in town for the Season and so you will doubtless have that pleasure – though that is hardly the word to describe any encounter with Maria.' He slowed the horses to turn in through the park gateway and they continued along the South Drive. Other carriages were out, their occupants seeing and being seen. They attracted not a few stares and she could see nudges being given and remarks being made. She was not sure whether it was the fine curricle and horses, so stylishly driven, or whether it was the handsome driver, or perhaps even the sight of Marmaduke bringing up the rear. 'They are gossips taking note,' he remarked off-handedly, touching his whip to the greys in order to overtake a slower vehicle. 'Ignore them.'

They remained out for above a half-hour and during that time he behaved in a perfectly charming manner, conversing pleasantly on various topics and on their return helping her down from the carriage, once again with great care for her ankle but with strict propriety.

'Shall you attend the Montagus' ball next week, do you suppose?'

'If I am able to.'

He bowed. 'Then we shall meet again there.'

She went indoors and paused at a window to watch him leave, the curricle bowling away fast down the street. She thought, with feelings that were very confused: heavens, how I have misjudged him.

'What I should like to know, Augusta, is what *precisely* are the means that you possess of persuading Lord Nicholas to offer for Charlotte?' Lady Craven, seated in the second most comfortable chair in Lady Fairfax's drawing room, spoke frankly and forcefully. She had known Augusta for too many years not to be aware of her capacity for dissimulation. The reply that she received however was a model of brevity and truth.

'I've told him I'll disinherit him if he does not.'

Lady Craven, taken aback, collected herself. 'You surely cannot expect me to approve a marriage based on a threat?'

'I fail to see why you should not. I told you, Nicholas will make an excellent husband, and father. He only needs encouragement.'

'*Encouragement!* That is indeed a fancy way of putting it. Coercion would be more appropriate. Really, Augusta ... I value Charlotte's well-being and happiness far too highly to allow any such alliance. And, in any case, I think it highly unlikely that she would ever accept your nephew's hand. She would not easily be deceived by blandishments. Why, she does not even *like* him.'

'I hear she rode home from the park with him on his horse.'

'How did you learn of that?'

'Have you forgotten how London thrives on tittle-tattle? And anything Nicholas does is good grist to the mill.'

'She had sprained her ankle and could not walk home,' Lady Craven said stiffly. 'It was perfectly innocent.'

'On her part, I dare say. But there is nothing innocent about Nicholas. He will have taken full advantage of the situation. Tongues will be wagging.'

'Oh, dear...'

'He has her dog, too. Follows him all over the place. Some strange mongrel – everyone knows it's hers. It's been taken for the latest rage and people are going about with the illest-bred curs they can find. Her name's being bandied from lip to lip, Sophia. They had far better be married and have done with it.'

Lady Craven calmed herself. 'You are deliberately exaggerating, Augusta. Things cannot have come to such a pass. I shall not be panicked into marrying my daughter off to your nephew. My first care is for her happiness and well-being.'

'He'll make her a consummate lover and that's not to be sneezed at.'

There was a small, gasping sound from the chair by the window but, engrossed in their discourse, neither of the two ladies noticed. Lady Craven cleared her throat. 'That is indelicate, Augusta.'

A ghost of a smile flickered across her old friend's face. 'It is a fact nonetheless, my dear Sophia. You are acquainted with my nephew, are you not? You know how he is. Use your imagination. Half the women in London are in love with him.'

Lady Craven recalled her own fluttering heart and swallowed. 'But Charlotte is *not*.'

'She soon will be. I guarantee it, if he has put his mind to it. She has grown up very sensible, I grant you – I warned him of that – so he will exert himself most particularly. She will find it quite hard to resist.'

Sophia Craven pondered the question for a

moment or two. 'Well, even if Charlotte *does* fall in love with your nephew, Augusta, *he* will not feel the same for her. How could he bring her happiness?'

'Personally, I do not see the necessity for a great attachment. Marriage does not require undying passion on both sides to succeed. Mutual respect will serve just as well. George and I did not greatly care for each other after a while, but respect endured and we were perfectly content. Nicholas is gentleman enough to respect his wife.'

Lady Craven shook her head stubbornly. 'I am still far from convinced that it could be a happy union. Charlotte is a country-loving girl. Fine looking, to be sure, but not a beauty. And she has none of the clever manners or style that Lord Nicholas must hold desirable. She does not care for fashion or Society, or gossip. Why she does not even care much for London.'

'Well, I offered him four other girls but he wasn't tempted by any of 'em. None of 'em holds a candle to Charlotte. It is my opinion that *she* is the one for him. She is his equal and much less likely to bore him, as so many do. He tires of them because they are all the same, and because the conquest is easy. If

Charlotte requires some effort on his part then it will only render her the more intriguing to him. We must hope that she withstands him for some appreciable time.'

'I hope that she will do so for ever. I must tell you, Augusta, that I am very reluctant to give my approval to the notion of this match. There are others whom I should infinitely prefer for Charlotte.'

'Who?'

'Well, there is Lord Petersham, for one.'

'A coxcomb.'

'And Mr Frederick Sparre.'

'A sadist.'

'Sir Andrew Edgeworth.'

'A nincompoop.'

'Lord Hervey.'

'A pervert. Who else?'

Lady Craven cast about in her mind.

'Lord Ranelagh.'

'A dullard.'

'Count Amarotti.'

Lady Fairfax waved her stick in special contempt. 'A foreigner! You don't mean to tell me, Sophia, that you would sooner see your daughter wed to any of those creatures? I know my nephew very well. For all his faults, he is capable of great kindness and tenderness. Charlotte would be neither ill-treated nor bored to death by him and that is a great advantage in a marriage. Picture what a handsome couple she and Nicholas would make. Imagine what fine children she would bear him.' Her ladyship paused cunningly. 'Your grandchildren.'

There was another sound from over by the window and this time Lady Craven was reminded of a third presence in the room. She cast an anxious glance at her friend. 'I do hope that none of this conversation will ever reach other ears than ours...'

'Snettisham has no ears,' her ladyship replied. 'Have you Snettisham?'

'Oh no, your ladyship.'

'Wouldn't keep her if she had. She knows that.'

'If Charlotte should learn the circum-stances she would *never* consent.'

'She will not learn them. Unless *you* tell her.'

'I? If I do, it will be to warn her.'

'Then consider this, Sophia. Between you and me. The day that Charlotte and Nicho-las are wed I shall move to the Dower House and make over Maplethorpe to him, together with a sizeable portion of his inheritance. He will come into the remainder when I die —which, to judge by my present state of health, will not be far off. Now what do you say?'

'This is barefaced bribery, Augusta.'

'But think how Charlotte will like Maplethorpe. You have often said yourself how much you admire it.'

That was perfectly true. In Lady Craven's opinion it was one of the loveliest old houses in England – not nearly as big or grand as some but infinitely charming and set in the most delightful countryside not many miles from her own dear home, which would be most felicitous. Charlotte would not be lost to them, as was so often the case in marriage. Far from it, they could visit regularly and see their grandchildren ... How much that would please Thomas, with Charlotte the very apple of his eye. Lady Craven took her leave presently and returned home, very thoughtfully, in her carriage.

Lady Fairfax addressed her silent companion. 'What *is* the matter with you, Snettisham? You look like a dying duck in a thunderstorm.'

'Nothing, your ladyship.'

'Are you ill?'

'Oh, no, indeed.' Miss Snettisham clasped feebly at her neck. 'The heat perhaps. It *is* a little oppressive today.'

'Heat? I do not feel it. Fetch me my shawl and kindly close the window.'

Seven

The Montagu Ball was one of the highlights of the Season and Mrs Beauclerc, *en grande tenue*, had taken unusual pains with her appearance. Her evening dress was of mauve silk, the edges of the overgown adorned with large gold Greek keys. She wore a fine piece of Brussels lace at her impressive bosom and on her head reposed a glittering diamanté bandeau set with curled ostrich feathers, dyed to match her gown and rising a good foot into the air. Mr Beauclerc, corseted as tightly as his wife in a similar, and vain, attempt to contain his girth, was squeezed into skintight buckskin trousers and a close-fitting coat and waistcoat, all of which constricted both movement and the ability to breathe. Buttons threatened to fly off at any moment. His lawn cravat, starched to a razor's edge, already chafed his neck before the evening had even begun, though his shoes had yet to trouble him, as had his gout. Their daughter was more simply and comfortably dressed in a white gown, her hair tied up on the top of her head and adorned with silk flowers, and curls twisting down on each side of her face. On their arrival, Mrs Beauclerc admonished her sternly.

'Should Captain Young be present this evening, Amelia, you are on no account to acknowledge him. You will certainly not exchange any words with him. And you most certainly will not dance with him.'

'Yes, Mama.'

'You mean, no, you will not, I trust. You may converse and dance with Lord Pomeroy as often as you please. Also with Lord Henry Vane and Sir John Westcomb – though not quite as much with Sir John. I shall inform you with whom else you may consort as the evening progresses. Ah, here is Lord Pomeroy. Remember to smile, Amelia, and say something witty.'

His lordship, extravagantly attired, advanced towards them. His cravat was tied in an elaborate bow with a veritable waterfall of ruffles down his chest and worn so high that his already insignificant chin had quite vanished. He was greeted with fawning civility by Mrs Beauclerc, indifference by her husband and reluctance by her daughter who failed to smile or make any remark, witty or otherwise. The honour of a dance having been requested, Amelia's parents watched her being led away.

'You see how attentive he is,' Mrs Beauclerc whispered behind her fan – also of matching ostrich feathers. 'Mark my words, he will offer for her soon.'

'I still think he's a fool.'

'What does that signify? Great intellect is not necessarily required in a husband. Amelia will be the Viscountess Pomeroy and that should be more than sufficient. But it will all come to nothing if she does not try harder to please. Just look at how *miserable* she appears.'

Mr Beauclerc, who had some sympathy with his daughter though he would not trouble himself to say so, grunted. Gout or no gout, he proposed to fortify himself against the long evening ahead with a quantity of claret and proceeded firmly in the direction of the refreshments, leaving his wife to her keen vigil.

★ ★ ★

'Miss Craven is here, Nicholas,' Captain Young remarked as he entered the ballroom with his friend. 'Her ankle must be better.'

'I imagine so.'

'You do not seem much interested. I thought you would be pleased to have the opportunity to further your suit.'

'I play my hand rather better than that, I hope, Clive. Since I had the good fortune to arrive like a knight errant to rescue the damsel in distress she has, unless I am much mistaken – and I am not usually mistaken about these things – revised her low opinion of me. The other day I called and took her for a carriage drive in the park, which gave me the opportunity for her to see again what a charming fellow I really am, and also for me to convey a hint of my admiration for her. She will be convinced of my interest and expect me to seek her out.'

'Well, she is over there, with Lady Craven. And looking very charming.'

'So she is.' Both gentlemen bowed in the direction of the two ladies.

'You are not going to ask her to dance?'

'Not yet. The longer I do not, the more she will desire it.'

'You can be monstrously unfeeling at

times, Nicholas.'

'If you have forgotten what is at stake, I have not. Miss Craven is no fool – that much I have learned in observing her; the game calls for rather more subtle play than usual, that is all.'

'How can you feign admiration where there is none? It would be impossible for me to do so.'

'I have always found it remarkably easy. And women are very gullible creatures in that respect. They will believe almost any compliment paid, even the most absurd.'

The two of them stood in silence for a while, watching the dancing until Captain Young caught sight of Miss Beauclerc partnering the viscount. He drew his friend's attention ruefully to the couple. 'What hope is there for me, Nicholas?'

'If it is any comfort to you, Clive, she looks anything but happy. I wonder if her mama is aware that Pomeroy is even more strapped than I? He lost six thousand pounds at faro the other night and finally emptied the family coffers. I'll wager his interest lies entirely in Miss Beauclerc's fortune.'

'Well, *I* cannot tell her of that.'

'The mother will doubtless learn it soon

enough. The question then will be how much she wishes her daughter to become a viscountess.'

The dance seemed to have lasted for hours. Amelia prayed for it to end soon so that she would no longer have to touch Lord Pomeroy's limp and moist hand whenever they came together. The thought of ever being married to him was too repugnant to contemplate and the longer the dance went on the more her resolve was strengthened: she would *never* consent to marry him, no matter what Mama did or said. Or Lord Henry Vane or Sir John Westcomb either. She would sooner die an old maid. At long last the music drew to a close with a final, tremulous chord from the fiddles. His lordship's finishing bow was so low and so prolonged that she was able to make her escape before he was aware of it, and to hide herself in among the crush. Mama would be incensed at such behaviour but, fortunately, she was engaged in conversation with a very grand lady wearing a great many jewels and, for the moment, too occupied to notice. Papa was nowhere to be seen. Amelia searched the throng, hoping against hope that she might chance on Captain Young and, just when she was about to give up and return meekly to Mama's side, she saw him near the entrance door with Lord Nicholas Strickland. He looked so fine and handsome in his military dress uniform that, just for a moment, she could only stand and stare until, conscious of precious time being lost, she hurried forward. His surprise and obvious pleasure at seeing her gave her further courage. She bobbed a curtsey to Lord Nicholas and wasted no further time on civilities.

'Captain Young, may we converse for a moment? Somewhere where Mama will not see us?'

They discovered a small adjoining room where a Chinese screen set across one corner provided a retreat. 'This is very forward of me, I know,' Amelia said. 'But I was so afraid that if I did not do something at once I might never be able to speak with you again. Mama has quite forbidden it, you see. I am not even to acknowledge you, much less speak to you. She believes you to be a fortune-hunter.'

'And do you believe that of me?'

'Of course I do not. But it is of no help

what *I* believe. *Her* mind is fixed. She takes no account of anything I say.'

The captain wrestled with his conscience. Miss Beauclerc was very young and it would be so easy for him to take advantage of her innocent trust. But how could he truly consider himself to be worthy of her when there were others of superior station and wealth whom she could marry to far greater advantage? The honourable course would be to respect Mrs Beauclerc's understandable amibition for her daughter. And yet, he could not bring himself to throw away this chance. He took her hands in his.

'Dear Miss Beauclerc, you do not know how greatly I value your trust in me and I swear to you that it is justified. Your having any fortune is a curse in my eyes not a blessing because it must drive a wedge between us.'

She said sadly, 'It is a curse in my eyes, too, because if I had none then I should not be troubled by gentlemen like Lord Pomeroy.'

He felt impelled then to warn her of what Nicholas had told him about the viscount's desperate financial straits. 'Oh, I guessed as much,' she replied. 'They cannot care for my face or my figure, so it must needs be for my fortune, which is a very depressing thing to know.'

'Why should they not care for you yourself? You are altogether lovely,' he told her passionately.

She shook her head. 'I know they do not. But it will not make any difference to Mama, so long as there is a title.'

'You must believe that my admiration for you is without motive. I could not bear you to doubt me, even for a moment.'

'Oh, I do believe you,' she answered. 'You are quite different from them. Different from anyone I have ever known. And if *I* trust and believe you then what does it matter what Mama and Papa and the whole world think? Can we not meet and talk in secret sometimes?'

'I should rather speak out honestly to your parents.'

'If you do then they will make very certain that we can never speak again. I beg you to do no such thing. Charlotte will help us. I am allowed to visit her and to walk in the park with her. I could send word...' A group of people entered the room at that point and Amelia turned pale. 'I must go back now. Mama will be searching for me everywhere.

Stay here for a moment longer so that we are not seen together.'

She was gone before he could speak another word.

In spite of the claret, or, more probably because of it, Mr Beauclerc's discomfort and discontent had increased considerably. His gout was plaguing him again – his right big toe, already under some pressure from his dancing pump, had begun to throb and his mood, uncertain from the very beginning of the evening, was deteriorating rapidly. He was vexed to see his wife descending wrathfully upon him, bringing further irritation.

'Where is Amelia?'

'I have no notion.'

'I have been searching everywhere for her; she is nowhere to be seen and Lord Henry is waiting to partner her in the next.'

'Then he will have to continue doing so if she is not to be found,' he growled.

Her bosom expanded in indignation, the Brussels lace rising like the foaming crest of a wave. 'How can you be so indifferent, Roland? Your daughter's future happiness is at stake.'

'It does not seem to me that Amelia's

happiness depends on whether she dances the next with his lordship or not.'

'You know very well what I mean. Lord Henry may be the younger son but ample provision has been made for him through the family trusts – I have made it my business to establish that. And, besides, who knows what may happen to his elder brother?'

'I trust you are not planning to arrange his early demise?'

'Do not be absurd. How could I be capable of such a thing?'

Very easily, Mr Beauclerc thought, though he did not actually voice this aloud. Another stab of pain came from his big toe and he grimaced and swore under his breath.

'I am merely making the point,' his wife continued, indifferent to his suffering – as always, 'that it frequently happens that, by some mischance of illness or accident the younger son inherits. In which case, Lord Henry would become an earl, whereas Lord Pomeroy is only a viscount.'

'What a dilemma that presents for you, my dear,' Mr Beauclerc remarked acidly. 'You have a viscount in the hand while the earl is only in the bush. What to do? What to do?'

'The first thing to be done is to find Amelia,' she retorted. 'For all we know she is consorting somewhere with that penniless captain.'

'No, she is not,' Mr Beauclerc replied. 'I can see her over there.'

'Where? Where is she? Show me at once.'

'Dancing with Lord Henry Vane. So you see, all your fussing and fretting was over nothing.'

Charlotte had been expecting Lord Nicholas to ask her for a dance, but as the evening wore on without him approaching she began to think she had been quite mistaken in the matter and found herself disappointed. He had, after all, been agreeable and amusing company when he had called and taken her out to the park and the same could not be said of many of the gentlemen present at the ball. She had danced with two very tedious partners who had nothing whatever of interest to say, another who had, by contrast, talked far too much – exclusively about himself – and with yet another so short of stature that she had felt like a giantess beside him. She had resigned herself to boredom and embarrassment when, quite suddenly, Lord

Nicholas appeared before her requesting the honour of a dance. She accepted with what she hoped was sufficient reticence, for it would never do to show the pleasure she truly felt. All her instincts warned her against it.

'I thought to find you claimed for every dance,' he said.

'By no means,' she answered. 'Gentlemen are put off by my height. They do not care to be looked down on. It makes them feel inferior.'

'How foolish of them. Superior height does not guarantee superior character. Nor the converse.'

'Very true,' she agreed. 'I believe that some of the greatest and most powerful men in history have been quite small. They say that the Emperor Napoleon, for one, is extremely short. Even so, I am thankful not to have had to dance with them. You do not know the awkwardness of it.'

'At least, you will be spared that with me.'

He was several inches taller and it was pleasant to have such a partner, as well as one who danced excellently. She knew that she did not perform so elegantly herself but she acquitted herself well enough, she hoped. And when he complimented her, she fancied that it was with some surprise on his part.

'Oh, I have had dozens of lessons with a French dancing master. Amelia and I have been the despair of the poor man but something, at least, was learned in the end. Occasionally I forget what I am meant to do next but I can usually get by without it being remarked.'

'I have not noticed a single mistake.'

'Then I must be improving for I am sure *you* would notice at once.'

'You believe me to be so critical?'

'Where female accomplishments are concerned, yes I do.'

They parted for the next section of the dance and when they were reunited he said, smiling at her, 'You are very severe on me, Lottie.'

His casual use of her childhood name disconcerted her for it implied an intimacy that had never existed between them. So did his smile. In fact, everything about him was disconcerting her. She had no idea how it had come about, but from disliking him so extremely she was in very grave danger of falling in love with him. At all costs, she

103

thought, I must conceal it for he would doubtless derive much amusement from the situation. 'I speak only as I find,' she said matter-of-factly. 'And, besides, your penchant for ladies of great beauty and style is well known. I cannot imagine you associating with a dowd. Be careful that you do not put that reputation at risk by dancing with me.'

Again, the dance parted them and gave him no chance to reply until later when they rejoined each other and she saw that he had been much diverted by her remark.

'My reputation could only be improved by being seen with you. I beg you never to deny me the pleasure of partnering you.' As he spoke, he was holding her hand and touched it to his mouth for the briefest second before releasing it and moving away from her in the dance. The next time they joined hands, it was an effort for her to enquire calmly after Marmaduke.

'He is very well,' Lord Nicholas replied. 'But his manners are still by no means all that they should be. You will have to entrust him to me for a while longer.'

'If you believe it necessary.'

'It is necessary if you want your mama to

allow you to keep him. Of course, you can see him whenever you care to. You have only to ask. Perhaps you would like to take another drive out in the Park tomorrow? Marmaduke would provide our escort. He has learned to follow me very obediently everywhere. Would you like that?'

She was saved from answering him immediately by the intricacies of the dance but she knew that she would like it very much.

Augusta Fairfax, dressed over all in the Fairfax emeralds, like a flagship, was ensconced on a comfortable sofa with Lady Craven in a corner of the ballroom. From time to time she put up her lorgnettes, the better to observe the scene. She dug her friend in the ribs with her elbow. 'Nicholas is busy charming your daughter and if I'm not mistaken it's working, Sophia. He's got her blushing like a milkmaid.'

Lady Craven was almost as short-sighted as Lady Fairfax but loathe to advertise or admit the fact. She peered at the fuzzy figures circling the floor. 'Where are they?'

'There, coming down the dance towards us now. Can you not see how taken she is?'

Lady Craven could not, for her daughter

was only a blur. 'You are imagining it, Augusta.'

'Indeed I am not. I know that look too well. I told you she'd find it hard to resist him. I only hope she doesn't make it too easy for Nicholas.'

Lady Craven bridled indignantly. 'I should hardly describe Charlotte as easy. She is nothing of the kind. And I am still far from convinced that this whole idea is in the least sensible.'

'Nonsense, it's the most sensible thing we've ever thought of. And you already agreed, Sophia, so there's no weasling out now.'

Lady Craven had no recollection of doing any such precise thing as agreeing, but she held her tongue. Her daughter and Lord Nicholas had moved close enough now for her to perceive them more clearly and she saw what a very fine couple they made. Charlotte's face and expression were still rather indistinct but she could readily believe that she was succumbing to the handsome figure at her side. Her ladyship fanned herself vigorously. She would have found it quite difficult to resist, herself.

'Miss Craven? We have not met before but I believe you are acquainted with my husband's aunt, Lady Fairfax?' Charlotte turned to see a thin and sharp-featured woman addressing her. The stranger was dressed in a magenta gown that did not become her either in colour or style, but with enough jewels hung about her to serve as some distraction from her looks, while testifying to her high station. 'I am Maria Strickland. My husband, Edwin, is the earl. I noticed you dancing just now with his younger brother, Lord Nicholas. He makes a charming partner, does he not?'

'He dances very well.'

'It is one of the talents he employs to entice the unwary.' The countess took her arm. 'My dear Miss Craven, may we talk privately for a moment? There is something of *great* importance that I should tell you.'

Charlotte found herself being ushered willy-nilly away from the main throng of guests and into a far corner of the room sufficiently distant from the orchestra to make conversation more audible. The countess let go of her arm. 'I must warn you, Miss Craven.'

'Warn me? Of what?'

'Of my brother-in-law, Lord Nicholas.'

She replied with some asperity, 'I am well aware of his reputation, Lady Strickland. There is no need to warn me.'

'His reputation for philandering is bad enough, Miss Craven, and richly merited. But, unfortunately, that is by no means all. I was visiting Lady Fairfax a few days ago and, quite by chance, exchanged some words with her companion, a Miss Nettlesham. You are acquainted with her?'

'I am afraid not. I believe she has only been with Lady Fairfax for a short while. There were other companions before.'

'Quite so. And this one is of no more significance than the rest. A very dull person. I should scarcely have noticed her, and certainly not entered into any conversation, had it not been a question of civility since we were left alone together for some time. I believe I made some casual remark where-upon she poured out this *extraordinary* story concerning Nicholas. Of course, she should not have told me but I was quite powerless to stop her.'

'I should much rather not hear it.'

'Oh, I think you should. It concerns you, you see.'

'*Me?* How can it?'

'Allow me to explain further, Miss Craven. At first I resolved to say nothing to a living soul, but since then my conscience has troubled me greatly and I have reached the conclusion that it is my Christian duty to warn you of the danger you are in.'

'*Danger?*'

'Danger of being grossly deceived. Of great personal unhappiness.' The countess gripped her arm again. 'Are you aware that Nicholas is the sole heir to Lady Fairfax's estate, including her country seat Maplethorpe?'

'No, I am not. And I cannot see that this concerns me in the least.'

'But it *does*, Miss Craven, I assure you. Miss Nettleton informed me that she heard an exchange between her employer and Nicholas when he was visiting and she was in the room. Lady Fairfax has become so disenchanted with Nicholas's spendthrift and loose behaviour that she has decided to disinherit him. To write him out of her will!'

Charlotte tugged her arm free. 'I really should much rather not hear this, Lady Strickland. It is surely a very private affair and none of my business.' She began to move away.

'Wait! You have not heard the whole of it. There was one condition for not doing so. One way for Nicholas to remain her heir. Lady Fairfax informed him that if he married suitably within the year she would reconsider her decision. She apparently believes that a sensible marriage will cause him to mend his ways and to settle down. How little she must know Nicholas! She even specified whom the bride was to be.'

Charlotte paused. 'Who?'

'You, Miss Craven. You are the chosen bride. If Nicholas marries you then the will stands.'

She found her voice after a moment. 'And what did Lord Nicholas say to that?'

'According to the companion person, he refused completely, at first. Lady Fairfax later offered him a choice of four other eligible brides, but none could tempt him. I imagine that he did not believe that his aunt truly meant it. He will have counted on charming her out of her displeasure, as he has always done in the past. But now it is clear that he has realised that she fully intends to carry out her threat. He will be near penniless without his inheritance, you see. He has squandered everything on gambling and high living. Unless he marries you, or one of the other four, he faces a bleak future indeed. And, of course, he has always liked Maplethorpe and considered it as his own.' The countess gave a vinegary smile. 'That is why he has been so *very* attentive to you, Miss Craven. Do not, for one moment, imagine that it is for yourself. His taste in women is altogether different, I assure you. You are Lady Fairfax's first choice. Marriage to you would instantly secure his inheritance. His sole aim is to make you fall in love with him and accept a proposal. If I had not warned you, he might well have succeeded in perpetrating this vile deception and you would have spent the rest of your days with a husband who cares not a jot for you. Only for himself.'

What a simpleton she had been! How could she ever have supposed that such a man would have been in the least attracted by her? Had he any inkling of how close he had been to success? She prayed to God that he had not. Prayed that she had not betrayed her growing feelings for him by any word or look so that she might keep her dignity in the whole affair. And at all costs he must not learn that she had discovered the truth. She must continue as though she knew nothing. And why not pretend to be enamoured – even besotted, for good measure – so that she might have the infinite pleasure of refusing him when he finally asked her hand in marriage? Two could play at the game of deception.

She said very calmly, 'Thank you for telling me, Lady Strickland. I trust that this interchange will remain between you and me and that nobody else will come to hear of it.'

'My dear Miss Craven,' the countess gave another thin-lipped smile. 'I assure you that the secret is quite safe with me.'

Eight

The heat in London was intolerable. Every ball and assembly became a Turkish bath. Ladies fanned themselves to no avail, and gentlemen cursed *sotto voce* as they mopped their dripping brows. The grass in the parks turned brown and Rotten Row became a dustbowl. The only relief to be found was in the shade of the trees where Charlotte and Amelia walked whenever the opportunity arose. At first, Charlotte had kept her discovery about Lord Nicholas to herself and she was obliged to listen to Amelia's opining that his lordship was likely to propose at any moment – certainly before the Season was out.

'In my view, Lottie, there can be no doubt about his feelings. To be sure he is discreet, but I have watched the way he attends to you. I have seen the way he speaks to you and the way he smiles at you. You have captured his heart and that is no mean feat, you know. They say that no woman has ever achieved that before.'

'You are quite mistaken. I have done nothing of the kind, Amelia.'

'Oh, but you have ... I can tell. And I can tell that you are by no means indifferent to him. Well, who could be? He is so very handsome and charming. If it were not for my dear Captain Young, I should be far from indifferent myself – though of course Lord Nicholas has never shown the least interest in me, so the question would never have arisen.'

Charlotte stopped walking. 'It is time that I disabused you of any such notion, Amelia. Lord Nicholas is pretending. He is not in the least little bit in love with me.'

Amelia stopped, too, and stared, open mouthed. 'But why should he pretend to be?'

Charlotte related what the Countess of Strickland had told her. 'But you are not to say a word to a living soul, promise me? And especially not to Captain Young. He very likely knows all about it, being such a good friend of Lord Nicholas. I do not wish Lord Nicholas to learn that I am perfectly aware of his situation. I want him to believe that I am simpleton enough to have fallen hook, line and sinker for his charm. It will give me the greatest pleasure and satisfaction to refuse him when he finally proposes.'

Amelia's face had fallen. 'Oh, what a disappointment...'

'What do you mean? Why should it be so?'

'I was *so* happy for you, Lottie. Quite convinced that you had found the ideal husband – for you are rather hard to please, you know. I was sure that Lord Nicholas admired you deeply. Are you really *certain* that it is all a sham?'

'How could it be otherwise? You know very well what kind of company he keeps. Is it likely that *I* would be of the very least interest to him unless he had an ulterior motive?'

'I suppose not. But I'm still disappointed.'

'Well, I am not, I assure you.'

'I thought that you had truly begun to care for him?'

'Care for such a man as he? He is dishonest and vile and utterly despicable.'

'I can see that you are very angry with him.'

'How could he stoop so low? How could he

be so treacherous? I cannot wait to see his face when he learns that his plan has not succeeded after all.'

She did not have long to wait before seeing Lord Nicholas's face again since he called the very next day and was shown into the drawingroom where she was sitting with Mama, frowning over a piece of embroidery. Somehow she had never mastered the art of making small, neat stitches and the thread frequently became knotted as she worked. She was just trying to disentangle it yet again when his lordship was announced. Her heart beat a little faster at the sight of him but this, she reminded herself, was only in anticipation of the role she must act in deceiving him. And it was so very satisfying to string him along a little, to oblige him to bestir himself to make extra efforts that he was doubtless unaccustomed to doing. Accordingly, she smiled at him, but not too much.

Her mother, on the other hand, was all graciousness to their visitor and displayed none of the guarded manner she had once adopted towards him.

'We are very pleased to have your company, Lord Nicholas, are we not, Charlotte? I was just saying how dull the day seemed.'

'Were you, Mama?'

'Perhaps you were not listening, my dear, being so preoccupied with your embroidery.'

The knot was refusing to come untied, despite Charlotte's covert attempts. As she tugged in vain, Lord Nicholas came closer, the better to see her work. He surveyed it in silence for a moment before he observed, with a slight smile about the corners of his mouth. 'I can see why it requires your full attention, Lottie.'

'Unfortunately, needlework does not come naturally to Charlotte,' Lady Craven confessed. 'But she is improving daily, is that not so, my love?'

'No, it is not, Mama, as Lord Nicholas can tell very clearly from where he is standing.'

His smile grew wider. 'Personally, even the finest embroidery does not interest me greatly. I admire it, of course, but deplore the number of hours the embroiderer must necessarily spend with her head bent low and her eyes cast down when she might be observing all else that goes on in the world around her. I should advise you not to persevere too hard, if I were you, Lottie. There is so much else to enjoy. For instance a ride out in the park in my carriage – with your permission, Lady Craven.'

Her ladyship demurred. 'Surely it is rather hot outside?'

'There is a pleasant breeze today and I promise to keep the carriage in the shade of the trees as much as possible.'

'In that case ... You would enjoy it, I dare say, Charlotte. You are always fretting at being confined indoors so much here in London.'

'I should finish this though, Mama.'

'Nonsense, my dear. As Lord Nicholas rightly says, there are other things in life beside embroidery. The outing will do you good. You have been looking quite pale of late.'

If Charlotte had not known it to be unlikely in the extreme, she might have suspected her mother of encouraging the match. Mama had always preached extreme caution where Lord Nicholas was concerned and she could not imagine why she had given her approval. It was very curious, but if she were to pursue her objective there was no alternative but to pretend enthusiasm herself. She laid down the tangled embroidery. 'Perhaps you are right, Mama. I should like to take some air.'

To her great pleasure, Marmaduke was waiting outside beside the same elegant carriage and two greys. She was rather surprised that the fine equipage, won by gambling, had not long since been lost in the same way, but she refrained from comment. She patted the dog and fondled his floppy ears, relieved to see how fit and content he looked, and amazed at how well-behaved he had miraculously become. Instead of leaping up and all but knocking her to the ground, he stayed sitting quietly where he was. Lord Nicholas handed her up on to the seat. She settled herself and opened her parasol against the sun. There was, indeed, a lovely breeze and once they had gained the park, he kept to his word and turned the horses towards the cool shade of the plane trees, slowing them to a gentle walking pace. She turned her head to see that Marmaduke was following obediently a short way behind.

'I must thank you for his good behaviour,' she said, obliged to give him the credit, at least, for that. 'Mama will not object to his return now, I am sure.'

'Oh, he's not quite ready yet,' he answered. 'There are still lessons that he must learn.'

'I miss him.'

'Then we must make certain that you are able to see him as often as possible. Unfortunately, of course, that will also involve seeing me. I trust you do not find that too abhorrent a notion.' She declined to answer and he went on. 'You know, I have been hoping that your poor opinion of me from childhood had altered, Lottie.' She pretended to be engaged then in watching some deer grazing nearby and he reined in the horses still slower and said softly, 'My opinion of *you* in those days has altered beyond recognition. I now find you one of the most captivating and interesting women I have ever met.'

In spite of herself, she blushed. She said with feigned archness: 'You don't speak of beauty, I notice.'

'You would not believe me if I did. Beautiful you are not – at least not in the conventional way of so many women that may be seen about London any day. You are something rather more than that. Something that arrests attention more than mere prettiness; something that endures for ever.'

What a devil he is, she thought. If I did not know that he was lying through his teeth, I might so easily be fooled by such smooth flattery.

He was smiling his most charming smile at her. 'I can see by the look on your face, Lottie, that you don't believe a word that I'm saying.'

'Well, I have no doubt that you speak in a similar fashion to most women. It is simply your habit. What puzzles me is why you should trouble to do so to me.'

'Because I mean it, therefore it is no trouble. Quite the contrary. Perhaps, by and by, you may come to believe me – when you know me better.'

'I hardly think that likely.'

'That you will ever believe me? Or that you will come to know me better?'

'Both,' she said firmly, mindful of her plan to make it quite difficult for him.

'Have you not revised your opinion at all of me?' he persisted. 'Or at least begun to do so?'

'Oh yes.'

'I am glad to hear it.'

'I did not say in which direction.'

He laughed at that. 'Perhaps it's for the worse, in which case I should be exceedingly sorry. As I am sorry for behaving so poorly to you all those years ago when you were a little girl. Was I really so unpleasant?'

'It seemed so to me.'

'I can recall so little of the occasions when we met. Am I right that you came to Maplethorpe with your mama?'

'Yes. You were obliged to play a game of ludo with me.'

'I take it that I won?'

'No, you lost.'

He clicked his tongue. 'I could not have been attending. I usually win at all games.'

'It made you even more disagreeable. You sulked.'

'How tedious for you. I can only apologize. Tell me, what did you think of Maplethorpe?'

'I think I thought that it was very beautiful.'

'It is, indeed. The most beautiful place on earth, to my mind. I love it dearly.'

She realized from his tone of voice and the expression on his face that his feeling for the property was, at least, perfectly sincere and true. It explained, though it did not remotely excuse, why he was prepared to go to such lengths not to lose it. When he delivered her back to the house she allowed him to hand her down from the carriage with closer attention than was strictly necessary and, on parting with him, gave him, with a sidelong smile, to understand that she would not be completely averse to him calling again soon.

Nine

'Lottie, Captain Young and I are to meet in the park today at eleven o'clock to take a walk. Please say you will come with me, as chaperone, so that it will all be respectable.'

'Your mama would not like that, Amelia.'

'She will not know. It has been arranged in secret. Kitty, our parlour maid, took a letter from me to the captain and brought his reply. Since Mama forbids me to see him it's the only way we can meet and I shall *die* if I cannot be with him again. He is the most wonderful, perfect gentleman in the world, you know, and wishes that I were poor so that my fortune would not stand between us.'

'Do you believe him?'

'Of course I believe him. Why should I not? He is honourable and good and true.'

'He is also a friend of Lord Nicholas and think how *he* is deceiving me.'

'Oh, Captain Young is not in the very least like Lord Nicholas. They are quite different. Surely you can tell that, Lottie?'

'He does seem very different, that's true.'

'So, you will come to the park this morning with me?'

'Very well. But I do hope you are right about him, Amelia.'

The two of them set off to walk the short distance to Hyde Park. The weather had cooled a little and a shower of rain had refreshed both the air and the dried-up grass. 'We are to meet on the east side of the Serpentine,' Amelia said. 'As though quite by chance. We must pretend to be very surprised to encounter him in case anyone is watching.'

But when she caught sight of the captain standing waiting by the bank, Amelia quite forgot to pretend at all and ran across the grass towards him, hands outstretched. 'Oh, Captain Young I am so very glad to see you again...'

He took her hands in his. 'And I you, Miss Beauclerc. I was afraid that you might not be able to come after all. But you are not alone, surely?'

'My friend, Miss Craven, accompanies me.

See, here she is. She knows our secret and you need not be afraid that she will tell a soul. Will you, Charlotte?'

'Of course not.'

The captain bowed. 'We are indebted to you, Miss Craven. Please be assured that the last thing I would wish is for Miss Beauclerc to come to any harm or distress on my account.'

'She knows that, don't you, Charlotte?'

She met the captain's eyes and searched in their depths for any sign of duplicity but could see only frankness and truth.

'I trust so.'

They began walking along the bank together and presently Charlotte lagged a little behind, stopping to pick a daisy here and there, so that the captain and Amelia might converse alone for a little. I pray, for Amelia's sake, that she is right about him, she thought. He appears all that she believes him to be and yet he is a friend of Lord Nicholas so how could he be completely honourable? Captain Young must very likely know all about Lord Nicholas's predicament over Maplethorpe. They would have discussed it together. Discussed herself, no doubt. A humiliating prospect. To be fair, though, she could not blame the captain for his friend's perfidy. And, observing the couple walking ahead of her, so blissfully happy in each other's company, she was more than ever convinced of Captain Young's sincerity. How will it end, though? she wondered anxiously. Amelia's mama will never permit such a match. Never in a thousand years.

'Lord Pomeroy is here to speak to you, Amelia.'

'Speak to me, Mama? What about?'

'What about? Marriage, of course. He has asked Papa's permission to address you, which, naturally, he has given, and all that is to be done now is for you to accept his offer.'

'But I do not wish to marry him, Mama.'

'Do not argue, Amelia. It is all arranged. A most suitable and satisfactory match. Lord Pomeroy is waiting in the drawing room. You will listen to what he has to say and then you will accept as soon as he has finished saying it.'

When she entered the drawing room the viscount was engaged in admiring his reflection in the gilt looking-glass above the mantel. So absorbed was he, that he did not, at first, notice her but continued for some time to observe himself this way and that and to make minute adjustments to the folds of his necktie. At last, he caught sight of her in the glass and turned, making her an exaggerated bow with great, twirling flourishes of his hand.

'Your servant, Miss Beauclerc. Allow me to say how charming you look and what extraordinary pleasure it gives me to see you.'

'Will you sit down, Lord Pomeroy?'

He seated himself with yet more flourishes of hands and fussy rearrangement of his coat-tails. Amelia sat down as far away as possible, consistent with good manners, and braced herself. He leaned forward.

'Miss Beauclerc, it cannot have escaped your attention that I have conceived an admiration for you – indeed, a *tendresse*. I have reached the conclusion that you would make a most charming and fitting Lady Pomeroy and, accordingly, your papa has given me consent to speak to you. I offer you my hand and heart and am confident that you will find me most worthy of your acceptance.' He brushed a speck of dust from his coat sleeve as he spoke.

Amelia took a deep breath. 'I am grateful to you, my lord, for your esteemed offer, but unfortunately I find myself unable to accept.'

He looked up from perusal of the offending sleeve with a slight frown. 'Unable? *Unable?* Surely not?'

'I do not love you, my lord.'

'Good gracious,' he looked startled. 'Pray do not let that concern you, Miss Beauclerc. Indeed, I should find it somewhat indelicate if you declared at once that you did. In my opinion, a wife's affection for her husband should come *after* marriage and should, in any case, always be modestly displayed. I cannot imagine anything more wearisome than a woman constantly hanging round one's neck.' He flicked at another speck on his breeches. 'So, with that small matter settled, I take it that we may now convey the happy news to your papa and mama?'

She leaped up, clasping her hands together. 'No, you may *not* take it as so, Lord Pomeroy. Not only do I not love you, but I do not wish to marry you under any circumstances. I could *never* come to care for you, nor do I believe that you truly care for me. Rather, it is my inheritance that you care for. Not me at all.'

He rose too, his painted face flushed.

129

'Permit me to say, Miss Beauclerc, that I find that remark insulting in the extreme.'

'I am sorry for it, indeed I am, but I believe it to be perfectly true. And it is better that we both understand each other immediately.' She was trembling and clasped her hands the tighter, collecting herself. 'I thank you for your offer, Lord Pomeroy, but I am obliged to decline. I wish you good fortune in finding a wife suited to your needs.'

He said waspishly: 'And I wish you fortune in finding a husband, Miss Beauclerc. In spite of the inheritance you so vulgarly refer to, you will not, I fear, meet with many gentlemen my equal in rank who will be prepared to overlook your deficiences in other respects. Believe me, *those* are manifold.' He gave her a curt bow without any of his customary flourishes and left the room with a toss of his head.

Her mama came hurrying in. 'I thought I heard Lord Pomeroy leaving. Surely he has not departed without speaking to us of your engagement?'

'He could not speak of it, Mama, for we are not engaged and never will be. I have refused him.'

'*Refused him!* What can you mean, Amelia?

Have you lost your senses?'

'No, I have found them, Mama. I do not love Lord Pomeroy. Indeed, I dislike him exceedingly. I should far sooner be dead than marry such an odious creature.'

'Do not talk such nonsense. You shall marry whom you are told. Lord Pomeroy is a most acceptable match and you are extremely fortunate to have an offer from a gentleman of his rank, considering your sad lack of accomplishments and looks.'

'Indeed, he told me the very same himself just now, Mama. And he was much put out to think that he will not, after all, be able to avail himself of my inheritence. He had counted on it, you know, to pay his debts. I hear they are quite considerable and he has gambled all his own family fortune away.'

'Gambled it away? *All* of it?'

'Yes, Mama. Every penny. Only last week he lost six thousand pounds at cards and that was the finish of it. And I do not suppose it would be very long before he did the same with mine.'

'I do not believe a word of it.'

'I assure it is true, Mama. And common gossip in London. I am astonished that it has not come to your own ears.'

Much disturbed, Mrs Beauclerc went in search of Mr Beauclerc and discovered him dozing peacefully in a wing-backed chair in the morning room, his gouty foot propped on a stool.

'Amelia has refused Lord Pomeroy.

He opened his eyes wearily. 'Has she? I can't say I blame her. The fellow's a fop and a fool.'

'He's more than that. He is penniless. Amelia tells me that he is an inveterate gambler. Last week he lost *six* thousand pounds at one sitting.'

'So I heard.'

'Why did you not say so, Roland? Why did you not tell me?'

'My dear Dorothea, you would not have listened. So long as he had a title, that was all that mattered – am I not right? Besides, I thought Amelia would have the sense to turn him down and so she has. Now, if you will excuse me, I was taking a nap...' He closed his eyes.

Mrs Beauclerc paced the floor – to and fro, to and fro. 'There is still Lord Henry Vane. Or perhaps it would be better to settle for Sir John Westcomb. Both would answer well enough. I think I am inclined to favour Sir

John. His family has been at Westcomb Park for over three hundred years, you know, and he is irreproachable.'

'He's dull as ditchwater.'

'There is nothing wrong with dullness, Roland. It is greatly to be preferred to profligacy. Yes, upon reflection I think, Sir John will do very well ... What do you say?'

Mr Beauclerc answered her with a gentle snore.

Ten

'Lord Nicholas has called, milady.'

'Thank you, Mason. You may show him in so long as he is sober.'

'He is, milady. Perfectly. Indeed, if I may say so it is some time since I saw him otherwise.'

'You may not say so, Mason. Just show him in.'

The butler bowed and presently Lord Nicholas strode into the drawing room. Miss Snettisham, who had raised her eyes shyly from her work, was rewarded by a bow and a flashing smile that caused her fingers to flutter at her throat. Lady Fairfax gave a snort.

'You seem in uncommonly good humour, Nicholas. Why, I wonder?'

He leaned against the mantelpiece, as usual, one booted foot propped on the fender. 'It's a fine day and I am in fine spirits, Aunt.'

'Huh. I hoped you might have some news of Miss Craven.'

'I have indeed.'

'She has accepted you?'

'No, I have not yet proposed.'

'It would certainly be somewhat premature. The child scarcely knows you and what little she does know is not pleasant. She will need time to be persuaded.'

He smiled. 'I am perfectly aware of it.'

'You've been driving out with her, I hear.'

'I have. And rather enjoyable it has been. She is not nearly as uninteresting as I first thought. She quite amuses me, in fact. And that's rare in a woman.'

'Do you amuse *her*, that is far more to the point.'

'I have been all that is charming to her.'

'I dare say, but she's no fool, Nicholas. Take care she doesn't start to mistrust you.'

'Why should she? She has no inkling of your diabolical scheme.'

'She's not the sort you usually pay court to. She knows that.'

'I have never found it in the least difficult to convince any woman of my sincere and abiding devotion. Lottie will be no exception. Wait and see. Before long she will be falling into my arms.'

Miss Snettisham gave a faint cry.

'What on earth is the matter, Snettisham?'

'I'm so sorry, milady. I pricked my finger.'

'How clumsy of you.'

'That is unfair, Aunt. Miss Snettisham is exceedingly *un*clumsy. She does the finest embroidery work that I have ever seen. Perhaps when Miss Craven and I are married you will undertake to teach her, Miss Snettisham. *She* does quite the worst that I have ever seen.'

'Oh yes indeed, of course, I should be delighted, Lord Nicholas. Delighted.'

Lady Fairfax rapped her cane sharply on the floor. 'You're turning her head again, Nicholas. Stop it at once. Miss Snettisham will do nothing of the kind. Charlotte's embroidering is not in the least important. She will have more than enough to occupy her when she is mistress of Maplethorpe. When do you see her next?'

'I am to take her to the zoo the day after tomorrow.'

'How bizarre. Whatever for?'

'She likes animals.'

'Huh. That appalling dog of hers ... is it still with you?'

'Certainly. He's rather a nice dog as it happens, now that he has learned some manners, and I have every intention of keeping him when we are married.'

'Don't count your chickens yet, Nicholas.'

He laughed. 'Dear Aunt, she is already halfway in love with me.'

'What am I to do now, Charlotte? No sooner did I contrive to be rid of that odious Lord Pomeroy than Mama has decided that I must marry Sir John Westcomb instead. He has called three times this week and I have nearly fallen asleep from boredom on every one. He sits there, scarcely uttering, and when he does speak it is about something *so* dull that there is nothing more to be said on the subject. His greatest passion in life is collecting moths, you know. Can you believe it? *Moths*! He says he has a whole room at Westcomb Park devoted to them. Hundreds and hundreds of the poor creatures stuck on pins in glass cases. I should feel so sorry for them. The last time he called, all he could talk of – when he did talk – was something called a bagworm moth that he had just acquired. It lives only two days, apparently, and the female lays her eggs in a sort of bag made of leaf and grass. He described it all in some detail to us. Mama thought it somewhat indelicate of him to mention such things.'

Charlotte laughed. 'Well, you must certainly not marry him, Amelia. To come a poor second to a collection of moths would not make for great happiness.'

'Oh, I have no intention of doing so. If I am to be married it must be to Captain Young, or nobody. But you know how persistent Mama is once she has set her mind to a thing. It is so very hard to stand up against her.'

'Then the only way is to discourage Sir John yourself. Persuade him that marriage to you would be a veritable disaster.'

'But how? I believe he quite likes me – though his feelings are always hard to tell.'

'Well, you say that moths are his great passion – above all else. So, next time you speak with him – out of your mama's hearing, of course – let him know that you cannot abide moths, or butterflies or winged insects of any kind and that you would be quite unable to endure having them in the house – alive or dead. Tell him the mere sight of one brings on violent hysterics and dangerous palpitations. That should answer the matter.'

Amelia clapped a hand to her mouth, giggling. 'Oh, Charlotte, what a clever notion! Thank you, thank you. I shall say so to him at the very first opportunity. How fortunate you are that Lord Nicholas is not dull. Not in the very least. I cannot imagine him ever conceiving a passion for a moth collection. Do you think he will propose to you soon?'

'Well, I'm certain that he is quite convinced that I am falling in love with him.'

'Well, I must confess that I might find it rather hard not to do so – if I were in your shoes, that is. And if it were not for my dear Captain Young.' Amelia sighed. 'It seems a great pity that you must refuse him in the end.'

'Would you have me accept a man who is deceiving me so disgracefully?' Charlotte said indignantly. 'How could you even think such a thing?'

'I know. Of course, you cannot. But it still seems a pity. He is so very handsome and charming that one almost overlooks the rest. When are you next to see him?'

'He is taking me to the zoo tomorrow.'

'Well, wild animals will be a great deal more interesting, I dare say, than moths.'

The Countess of Strickland was seriously alarmed. 'Something must be done, Edwin. At once.'

'About what?'

'About your brother, of course. I have it on good authority that he has been escorting Miss Craven about town. Only last week he took her to the zoological gardens. They were observed at the flamingo pool and I am told that she was actually appearing to *enjoy* his company.'

'Nothing unusual in that. Nicholas could always charm the ladies.'

'Well, *I* find it extraordinary, considering that she knows very well that he is only paying her attention because he must marry her to inherit Maplethorpe. If it were not so, he would not even glance her way. I warned her of his treacherous plan, but it seems she has fallen under his spell in spite of it.'

'Then there is nothing to be done.'

'On the contrary, I intend calling on Miss Craven today. It is very clear to me that she does not fully understand the extent of your brother's depravity. His intemperance, his gaming, his debauchery, his extravagance ... I must make it all clear to her. Warn her yet again and in no uncertain terms. Send for the carriage at once, Edwin. At all costs a marriage must be prevented between them.'

The countess found Miss Craven at home and, by good fortune, alone. She swept into the drawing room, smiling as graciously as she was able. 'My dear Miss Craven, forgive this intrusion but I have been in such a turmoil of anxiety that I felt I must come immediately to see you.'

'I am very sorry to hear that, Lady Strickland, but I am at a loss to know how I may help you.'

'I shall come straight to the point. The matter concerns my brother-in-law, Lord Nicholas.'

'You have already spoken to me on that subject, Lady Strickland.'

The countess inclined her head. 'Indeed, I have. As you know, I felt it my duty some time ago to warn you of the plot conceived by Lady Fairfax to coerce Lord Nicholas into marriage with you.'

'Yes, I remember very well.'

'It has come to my ears that my brother-in-law has persisted in his attentions – you have been seen quite frequently in his company. His ability to charm is, of course, notorious and I believe he can easily convince the gullible of his sincerity, but you must allow me to repeat my warning, Miss Craven. You cannot comprehend what a rogue he is. His behaviour over the past years has been nothing less than scandalous. Nothing but reckless living. The most unsuitable liaisons with loose women, drinking to excess, gambling all the night ... why, are you aware that he has lost thousands at a sitting and is constantly in debt?'

'Yes, I am perfectly aware of it.'

'And yet you continue to endure his company?'

'He is very pleasant company.'

The countess snorted through her beak of a nose. 'No doubt. He would make very sure to be so where you are concerned. He is all flattery and persuasion when he has something to gain but, believe me, Miss Craven, he holds you in no esteem whatever. He cannot bear the idea of losing Maplethorpe – that is all. For some peculiar reason, he has always had veritable passion for the place.'

'I take it from your tone, Lady Strickland, that you do not?'

'It is pleasant enough, to be sure, but needs *much* improvement. The rooms are far too rambling for my taste – all higgledy-piggledy with no elegance or style. It is altogether too old-fashioned and worn and *very* draughty. The west wing should certainly be removed, as well as a great deal else. Nicholas would likely insist that nothing whatever was changed but one could not live in it with any degree of comfort without considerable alteration, as you would soon discover.'

'Tell me, Lady Strickland, if Lord Nicholas does not inherit Maplethorpe, who will?'

'Why, my husband, of course. The earl. Which is as it should have been arranged in the first place – if Lady Fairfax had not been so blind where Nicholas is concerned. Fortunately, she has now come to her senses.' The countess rose and drew on her gloves. 'Well, I shall not detain you further, Miss Craven. I have done my duty. I am delighted that you are under no illusions about my brother-in-law and will have no intention of accepting him.'

'I did not say that, Lady Strickland.'

Her ladyship looked startled. 'But surely that is the case? Have you no pride? No care that he has no regard for you?'

'Nor did I imply that I would accept him.' Miss Craven continued calmly. 'I am very grateful to you for your great anxiety on my behalf but you must allow me to say that whatever happens between Lord Nicholas and myself concerns us and us alone.'

Two spots of colour appeared in the countess's sallow cheeks. She stared uneasily at the girl. Now that she saw her again, and more closely, she did not seem quite so plain as she had first thought. Far too tall, of course, but there was no denying that she carried herself well enough and her features were quite passable. A terrible suspicion came into her ladyship's mind – that Nicholas might be entertaining some kind of genuine infatuation. Then she dismissed it instantly. Miss Craven was a very far cry from his usual choice of female company. Underneath his feigned eagerness, he must be bored stiff by this innocent country mouse. Fortunately, the girl seemed nothing if not sensible. Intelligent, even. She could be in no further doubt about Nicholas and seemed to have grasped the situation perfectly. The countess took her leave, congratulating herself on having accomplished a delicate mission so well.

* ★ ★ ★

Amelia lost no time in putting the plan into action. At the very next ball when Sir John Westcomb approached to claim her for the gavotte she pleaded a dizzy attack and declared that she would sooner sit and talk with him. He looked pleased – too pleased for her liking – and they repaired to a corner of the room. She could see Mama watching closely from her vantage point on the other side and the wink of her emerald tiara as she nodded her approval. Sir John, as usual, said nothing and she was therefore free to lead the conversation in whatever direction she chose. She unfurled her ivory fan and batted it vigorously, drawing gasping breaths.

'Oh, dear, I really do not feel at all well. I'm afraid it is one of my attacks.'

He looked alarmed. 'Your attacks?'

'Yes, they can last for several hours. It is a great nuisance, but I cannot help it.'

'I am distressed to hear so, Miss Beauclerc. But what causes them? Is it the heat?'

'Insects,' she said, drawing more deep breaths and fanning herself more vigorously still. *Flying* insects. I have a great fear of them, you see. I have only to be in the same room with one and an attack begins

145

immediately.' Amelia clasped at her bosom – approximately where she believed her heart to be. 'I have dreadful palpitations – I can feel them now – and can scarcely breathe, and sometimes I faint.'

'You mean wasps or bees, I take it, Miss Beauclerc? They can certainly be quite alarming.'

'I do not care for either of those, it is true, but they do not instil in me the fear – the *terror* – that I feel if I find myself near an insect with large wings. Wings that *flutter*.'

He looked even more disturbed. 'I am sure you could not mean butterflies, for instance? They are quite harmless.'

'Oh yes, butterflies are one of the things I *most* dread. And moths too. Both bring on the most dreadful attacks. I cannot bear to be near them. It was a moth that brought on this very one earlier this evening. It must have come in through the open window and was fluttering round the candles. I all but fainted but fortunately Mama had her smelling salts to revive me.'

'But if they are dead – without any movement – then surely they could not affect you so?'

'Dead or alive, I cannot abide them in

either form. Why, even *speaking* of them starts my heart racing.' She clasped at her bosom again. 'When you were talking of your collection when you called on us the other day, I wanted to implore you to stop but that would have been impolite, of course.'

'I do beg your pardon,' he said, frowning. 'I had no notion that you felt so or I should never have raised the subject.' He hesitated for a moment, then went on in wary tones. 'Do you mean, Miss Beauclerc, that you could never live in any proximity to either butterlies or moths? That it would be quite impossible?'

She fannned herself so wildly that she almost hit him on his long nose. 'Quite impossible, Sir John. It would be the death of me I am sure. It is like an illness, you see. The doctor has warned me that great care must be taken to avoid bringing on an attack. So please do not even mention your collection again. And do not speak a word of butterflies or moths. Pray, let us talk immediately of something else.'

At that he lapsed into his customary silence and she sat demurely beside him watching the dancers executing the gavotte.

Across the room Mama was nodding her approval again. Amelia smiled.

Charlotte had partnered Captain Young in the gavotte and when it was finished he detained her for a moment.

'I wanted to thank you, Miss Craven, for your kindness in acting as chaperone to Miss Beauclerc. I hope you believed me when I said that I have nothing but her happiness and well-being in my mind and heart.'

'I do believe you, Captain Young,' she assured him, willing, in spite of herself, to give him the benefit of any doubts caused by his association with Lord Nicholas.

He looked grave. 'Thank you for that trust. I am afraid, though, that it is a hopeless cause that you champion. Mrs Beauclerc's mind is set against me. I dare not approach Amelia in public for fear of causing her trouble with her mama. At every ball I must watch while she is obliged to dance only with others. It is a great trial for us both. Look how she is sitting now with Sir John Whitcomb. I know she does not like him but that does not signify with her mother. She would have her marry him tomorrow.'

'You have nothing to fear concerning Sir

John,' Charlotte told him. 'He will not offer for Amelia, I can assure you.'

'How so? How could any man not wish to marry her?'

She smiled. 'Indeed. But, as I trust you Captain Young, you must trust *me* in this matter. He will not propose and not even Mrs Beauclerc can force him to do so.'

'You are quite certain of this?'

'Yes. Quite certain.'

'I hope you are right, Miss Craven. But, in any case, if Sir John does not, there will be others, also approved by Mrs Beauclerc. Lord Henry Vane, for instance.'

'You must not be discouraged, Captain Young. Mrs Beauclerc cannot force Amelia to marry someone she does not love.'

He shook his head. 'She is a very formidable mama, in my opinion. And Amelia is accustomed to obeying her.'

'I will do what I can to stiffen her resolve.'

He smiled gratefully. 'Thank you again. If there is any way in which I may be of service to you, Miss Craven, you have only to speak.'

The captain was so clearly an honourable man that she wondered again how he could consort with Lord Nicholas who, equally clearly, was not. She said artlessly: 'I have not seen your friend, Lord Nicholas, this evening. Is he not attending the ball?'

'I believe not. He has another engagement.'

She pretended to be downcast. 'Oh ... I had so hoped that he would be here.'

He hesitated. 'Miss Craven, I hope you will not think it grossly impertinent of me if I ask if you entertain any warm feelings for Lord Nicholas?'

She appeared suitably flustered. 'Well, he is certainly very agreeable to me...'

'I'm sure. Ladies usually find him so.' Captain Young looked uncomfortable. 'And you may believe me that he is not nearly the reprobate that he seems to be. There is another, altogether more worthy and gentler side to him.'

'I am glad to hear it.'

'But, nevertheless, I am concerned for you, Miss Craven. If you are in danger of losing your heart, I beg you to be very careful not also to lose your head.'

He knows very well about the plan, she thought, and must remain loyal to his friend, but at least he has tried to warn me to be on my guard. I am grateful to him for that. 'You need not worry, Captain Young, my head has always ruled my heart.'

He was looking over her shoulder. 'Why, here is Nicholas now, after all. He must have changed his mind.'

She turned to see Lord Nicholas at the entrance to the ballroom. His late arrival had caused a stir, she saw with some amusement. Heads were turning, eyes staring, fans were fluttering, tongues whispering. He seemed quite unaware, but she guessed that he was perfectly conscious of being the focus of attention and, indeed, she had to confess to herself that he merited it. Whereas other gentlemen looked uncomfortable or even absurd in their evening finery, his dark coat and trousers and pure white cravat were simplicity itself. The cut was exquisite, the fit perfect, the effect of effortless elegance and, unlike all the others who were for ever tugging and adjusting and fussing over their attire, he wore his without paying it the slightest attention, like a second skin. She watched him greeting people here and there and saw how eagerly they responded, especi-ally the ladies. If she had not known that he had no need of such a trick to draw attention, she might have suspected him of arriving late on purpose. Not once did he glance in her direction, and she wondered if he had sought to disappoint her by his absence and, therefore, to make her all the more glad to see him now. There was no ploy, she decided, that was too low for him.

Her partner for the next dance presented himself – an amiable young gentleman several inches shorter than her – and she went to take her place opposite him. Weaving her way through the dance she saw, out of the corner of her eye, that Lord Nicholas was in conversation with her mother and his aunt, Lady Fairfax, who were seated in a corner together, and she noted how Mama was smiling up at him. He could charm the birds from the trees if he chose, she thought in disgust. Another dance passed and then another and she was beginning to wonder if he had decided, after all, that Maplethorpe was not worth the pain of having to marry her, when suddenly he appeared before her during the interval.

'It would be useless to beg the favour of a dance, Lottie, for I am quite certain that your card is full, but perhaps we may talk a little.'

She gave a good impression of blushing confusion. 'If you wish, Lord Nicholas. What did you wish to talk about?'

'Anything *you* wish,' he said smiling. 'Not the heat, though. I refuse to talk any more about the heat. The subject bores me to death.'

'Very well, may we speak of Marmaduke? How is he?'

'Exceedingly fit.'

'I still miss him. How soon before he returns?'

'A while. He is making good progress but I should not wish him on you yet. I was talking with your mama just now and promised that I would not surrender him until his manners are impeccable.'

'I see. It seems to be taking a very long time, though.'

'His manners were unusually bad – as you will admit yourself. It takes time to correct them. But you may believe me that he is perfectly well and happy with me.'

'I am glad to hear it, but I should still like him back soon.'

He looked at her steadily. 'I can see that you are quite prepared to overlook all his failings and foibles. I envy Marmaduke such devotion. You must truly care for him.'

'I am very fond of him, it's true.'

'Then he is indeed a fortunate animal.'

The orchestra had returned from their refreshments and were gathering up their instruments. In a moment her next partner would claim her. He said: 'I have asked your mama if I may call on you tomorrow. Will you receive me, Lottie?'

She lowered her eyes. 'Yes, of course.'

As her partner approached, he bowed and walked away. He is going to propose, she thought triumphantly, so certain is he that I will accept him. What a shock he is going to have!

By the end of the ball Mrs Beauclerc found herself very out of sorts. Nothing had gone well and she said as much to Mr Beauclerc. He, by contrast, had brightened up now that the evening was almost over and release from the torture of stays and tight clothing was coming closer by the minute.

'I cannot see why you are so fussed, Dorothea. It was a ball like any other ball. They none of them go well, so far as I am concerned.'

She frowned. 'Surely you have noticed.'

'Noticed what?' As he had nodded off from time to time, he had, of course, noticed

154

nothing.

'Why Sir John, of course.'

'There's nothing to notice about the fellow.'

'He danced only once with Amelia.'

'I dare say that pleased her.'

'But he had requested two more dances. Amelia says he begged to be excused as he did not feel well and yet I distinctly saw him standing up later with that Saunders girl. You know, Lady Winthrop's granddaughter.'

'What of it? They are well suited. She has nothing to say either.'

'You know perfectly well what hopes I entertained. I was quite certain that it would not be long before Sir John offered for Amelia and now, quite suddenly, it appears that he has changed his mind. It is exceedingly ill-mannered and inconsiderate of him, in my opinion, not to mention a great waste of my time. The Season will be over before we know it and we have let two eligible suitors slip through our fingers.'

'*Your* fingers, Dorothea. I play no part in this.'

'Surely you wish her to marry well,' Mrs Beauclerc protested.

'I have yet to meet the man I should be

happy to see my daughter married to,' he said imperturbably.

Her bosom heaved in irritation. 'Well, there is still Lord Henry Vane. He will do very well.'

'Is his elder brother in poor health, then?'

'How should I know? I have never met him.'

'I thought perhaps he might be. If Lord Henry is to be seriously considered for Amelia, it must mean that there is now a strong possibility of him inheriting the earldom.'

'You are mocking me, Roland. I take that very ill.'

'No, my dear, I was perfectly serious.' Mr Beauclerc drew out his pocket watch and surveyed it with satisfaction. 'In any case, your matchmaking plans will have to wait until another day. It is time to go home.'

Eleven

On the day after the ball, Charlotte awaited Lord Nicholas's arrival in the drawing room. She tried to concentrate on her embroidery work – as usual in something of a tangle – but kept rehearsing in her mind how she would behave and what she would say to him. She must be careful to lead him to assume that she would accept at once, so that her refusal would be all the greater surprise to him. He must be made to feel all the humiliation of rejection – it was no more than he richly deserved. And on no account must she let him suspect that she knew all about his perfidy. He should believe that she had rejected him for himself alone.

When Clutterbuck announced his lordship her heart leaped and she found that her hands were shaking so that she could scarcely hold her needle steady. He entered the room with all his easy elegance and charm, bowing to Mama and to herself, looking as though nothing in the world caused him the slightest concern. Which is indeed the case, she thought grimly, since he is perfectly certain of my acceptance and of thereby securing both his fortune and his beloved Maplethorpe. While he conversed with Mama she kept her head down, lest he should read anything in her eyes to warn him, and persevered with her embroidery, hoping that he would not notice the way her fingers were trembling over the stitches. Of course, the thread soon knotted up and she had to stop to unravel it. Naturally, *that* did not escape his notice and she could see that he was much amused though he made no comment. Presently, after some talk of the weather and the continuing heat and of gossip of the previous night's ball, Mama rose and made an excuse to leave the room. He has fooled her completely, Charlotte concluded. From doubting his every word, she is now quite convinced of his sincerity. If only she knew...

He must have noticed the fingers, after all, because he immediately asked why she was so nervous. 'You have nothing to fear from me, Lottie,' he said in a gentle voice that all

158

but undid her resolve.

'I didn't suppose that I had,' she said brightly, jabbing her needle into her work.

'You trust me, then?'

'Of course. Why should I not?'

He didn't answer. Not even *he* has the gall to lie about that, she thought, tugging at her thread. Instead, after a moment, he said: 'Believe me, I have the highest regard for you and I am sorry if I have ever given you offence or caused you pain in the past.'

'Oh, the past is past,' she said, smiling sweetly up at him.

'I am very glad to hear you say that, but it is the future that I am thinking of.'

'Oh?' She was all innocence, lowering her eyes, even managing a blush. 'What can you mean?'

'You know very well what I mean, Lottie, so let's not beat about the bush. I called on your papa in the country recently to seek his permission to address you, which he was good enough to give. I am asking you to do me the great honour of becoming my wife. I know that I must seem a very poor bargain but I swear I will do all that I can to make you happy. You would find me a devoted and considerate husband.' He had spoken with such apparent honesty that she could almost have believed him. Indeed, when she lifted her head he was looking at her in a way that made her blush deeper and, for a moment, she completely forgot her carefully rehearsed words. 'Have you nothing to say to me?' he went on. 'No answer to give?'

She pulled herself together; remembered her little speech, so carefully composed, so well rehearsed. 'I thank you for your offer, my lord, indeed I do, but regret that I must decline it.'

Instead of looking astonished, he appeared rather diverted. 'Come now, Lottie, that won't do at all. You must give me a reason.'

'I do not love you. That is my reason.'

He smiled slowly. 'But you would learn to do so, I promise.'

'And you do not love me.'

'I would learn to do that too. We would start with a great advantage over others, you know. We are neither of us so besotted with the other that it would inevitably end in unhappy disillusionment. We have known each other since childhood and both of us has a clear head and a clear eye and no illusions whatever. I fancy that we should do very well together. I have thought so for some time. And so have you, unless I am much mistaken. So, there is no need for this maidenly hesitation.'

It was not going at all how she had planned. Not at all. She had meant him to be angry, resentful, disbelieving, crushed, even – never amused. She drew herself up tall on the sofa. 'I assure you that it is not hesitation on my part, but complete certainty. I do not think we should do at all well together and I do not want to marry you. You have been quite mistaken in thinking that I wished it and I am sorry to have given that impression. It was quite unintentional.'

He raised an eyebrow. 'Unintentional? Was it? Are you telling me the truth, Charlotte?'

She met his gaze. 'Are *you*, my lord?'

There was a short silence. He said quietly: 'There seems little purpose in continuing this discussion now. You have refused my offer and that is all there is to be said for the moment. I shall hope that one day you will change your mind.'

'Pray do not hope any such thing, for I shan't.'

'You are quite determined, I can see.'

She turned her head away. 'Quite determined.'

'Then I shall not embarrass you by remaining any longer.' He came forward and took her hand in his, raising it briefly to his lips. 'I hope you will allow me to keep Marmaduke for a while longer. He still has lessons to learn and, in any case, I have grown quite fond of him.'

She took her hand away quickly. 'If you wish. But I should like him back soon.'

'You shall have him.' He looked down at her for a moment. 'You are quite wrong, you know, Lottie. We should do remarkably well together. And you would be very happy with me. Think upon it.'

He left the room and she hurled her embroidery at the door as it closed behind him. How monstrously arrogant he had been! How maddeningly calm! He had not seemed in the least shocked, as she had expected. Not in the least put out, let alone put down, as she had so hoped. And somehow, in spite of all her careful rehearsing, he had had the last word.

'She refused me, Aunt Augusta. Turned me down flat. She does not wish to marry me.'

Lady Fairfax looked up at her nephew, who was leaning against the mantelpiece; he seemed quite unruffled by his rejection. 'Indeed. And did she say why?'

'She does not love me and she does not believe that I love her.'

Her ladyship frowned. 'It's not like you, Nicholas, to fail on either of those counts. I'd swear the girl was in love with you. She looked head-over-heels to me.'

'Only pretending to be so, I fear.'

'*Pretending?* Why should she do that?'

'Perhaps she wanted to teach me a lesson ... Perhaps she doubted me from the very first.'

'Huh! I told you she was no fool. But she could not have known about the rest of it.'

'I wonder ... Did you speak of it to anybody else?'

'Certainly not.' Lady Fairfax had no intention of betraying her fellow-conspirator, Lady Craven. 'What do you take me for?'

'A ruthless, scheming old lady, my dear aunt,' he told her pleasantly. 'Are you positive that no one else could have known?'

'How could they? There was nobody else in the room but us when we discussed the matter.' They both looked at Miss Snettisham, who was desperately engaged on her needlework in her corner chair, head bent.

'At least, only Snettisham and she doesn't count. She would never breathe a word – she wouldn't dare. Would you, Snettisham?'

There was a gasp from the corner. 'Oh, indeed, no, your ladyship! Not a word.'

'I should hope not.' Lady Fairfax tapped her stick hard against the floor. 'So, Nicholas, if at first you don't succeed try and try again. You must exert yourself more with Miss Craven. You have never failed with any other ladies, so far as I am aware.'

'None of the ladies in question has ever been in the least like Charlotte,' he pointed out drily. 'You have always said as much yourself.'

'Which is precisely why she would be eminently suitable. I am surprised to see you so little offended by your rejection, considering that it is the first time any woman has denied you.'

'I admit that I had expected to be accepted, but it intrigues rather than offends me.'

'Well, intrigued or not, I am still set upon your marrying Charlotte Craven if you wish to inherit Maplethorpe. I have not altered my decision.'

'I did not imagine that you would, Aunt. And the irony is that I am no longer so averse to the notion myself. Charlotte, though, is, unfortunately.'

'Change her mind, then.'

He said languidly and with a smile: 'Oh, I intend to.'

When his lordship had left, Lady Fairfax glanced sharply at her companion, who was sewing away with great concentration. 'You are quite certain that you have not spoken to *anybody*, Snettisham.'

'Not a *soul*, milady.'

'If I discover that your tongue has been wagging...'

Miss Snettisham cringed. 'Indeed it has not, milady.'

'Humph!' Lady Fairfax tugged fretfully at the shawl round her shoulders. 'Well, pull the bell for Mason. He must send for the carriage immediately. I am going to call on Lady Craven.'

'What is to be done now, Augusta? Charlotte says that she will *never* change her mind. She says that Nicholas is the last man on earth that she would ever choose to marry.' Lady Craven had sunk on to a couch in the drawing room and was sniffing at her salts. 'It has all been quite upsetting.'

'Pull yourself together, Sophia. All is by no means lost. Nicholas has no intention of giving up and nor have I. Where is Charlotte? I intend to speak to her on the subject.'

'She is in the garden, but pray be careful what you say, Augusta. If she should ever suspect that we have plotted this together...'

'Don't be ridiculous. How could she think any such thing? Leave me with her for a few moments, that is all.'

Lady Fairfax found Charlotte sitting at the end of the garden beneath a tree and greeted her affectionately. 'My dear child, I shall come straight to the point. I hear that you have refused an offer from my nephew, Nicholas.'

'Indeed I have, Lady Fairfax.'

'I cannot blame you for doubting his worth – on the surface, he appears to be a thoroughly degenerate and faithless young man – but you should know that he has some most redeeming features.'

'I am very surprised to hear it.'

'I have known him since the day he was born. Indeed he spent a great deal of his childhood at Maplethorpe, as of course you are aware, so I can speak with some authority on the subject. For all his faults –

which I concede are many – beneath them lies a gentle and sweet and generous nature which would make a most delightful husband. There is no malice in him. No cruelty. None of that casual indifference towards women displayed by so many gentlemen, not to mention their deplorable deficiencies in the bedchamber.' Her ladyship plunged on regardless of the blush rising in her listener's cheeks. 'Quite the contrary. If I may put it rather bluntly, you would find him expert in that department. While it is by no means a necessity, it is certainly an added bonus in a marriage. The majority of women are not so fortunate, myself included. Most important of all, though, he would never – not for one second – bore you.'

Charlotte swallowed. 'What you say may be true, Lady Fairfax, but I still do not wish to marry him. And I wonder why he wishes to marry me, since he does not love me.'

'He may, or he may not. But he certainly respects you, my dear, and believe me that is worth a great deal more than any passing infatuation. Love may fade. If deserved, respect will remain and grow with the passing years. You would be the making of him and it would be a most satisfactory match. I hope that you will not entirely reject the possibility.'

'I am very sorry to disappoint you but I think it most unlikely that I shall ever change my mind.'

Lady Fairfax concealed a smile. 'I wouldn't be quite so certain, dear child. Nicholas can be extremely persuasive.'

'I dare say but I'm afraid that I am completely immune to all his charms.'

'Completely? Are you quite sure of that – it's quite rare, you know.'

'Completely.'

'No wonder he is so captivated.'

'Captivated?'

'Oh yes. Intrigued was the word he used, but it amounts to the same thing. You are quite different, you see.' Lady Fairfax patted Charlotte's hand. 'Of course, your refusal will have done him the world of good – there's no denying it – but I urge you to bear in mind what I have said. Believe me, my nephew would make you exceedingly happy.'

She took her leave and Charlotte sat for a while in the garden, thinking. She had no doubt that Lady Fairfax was genuinely fond of Lord Nicholas and saw some worth in him – just as Captain Young had claimed there to be. She had seemed perfectly sincere when speaking in his defence and, no doubt, was anxious to see him settled with a wife in the hope of curbing his libertine ways. But that did not alter the fact that the proposal had been a plot. And if it had not been for the countess – unpleasant though she undoubtedly was – she might very easily have been completely deceived and found herself married to a man whose only thought was his inheritance and who cared nothing whatever for his wife. She did not believe that Lord Nicholas was captivated. Not for a second. If he had persuaded his aunt that it was so, then it had only been to convince her, in his duplicitous way, that there was still some prospect of success. To stay her hand lest she summon her lawyers to change her will immediately in favour of his elder brother.

Charlotte sighed. It would certainly be a great shame if beautiful old Maplethorpe were to fall into the improving hands of the countess – for a wing to be knocked down and brutal changes to be made in the name of her notion of elegance and style – but there was nothing to be done about it.

Twelve

'You are to wear your blue silk today, Amelia.'

'Why, Mama?'

'It is your most flattering gown, in my opinion. It makes you seem a great deal slimmer. And Lord Henry and his mother are calling on us, in case you had forgotten. It is all arranged. I want you to look your best.'

'What for, Mama?'

'You know perfectly well. Lord Henry has been paying you marked attention of late and, since Sir John appears to have had his head completely turned by that sly Miss Saunders, it is advisable to give him every encouragement. The Season will soon be over and he may be your last chance to secure an acceptable offer.'

'I dislike him intensely, Mama.'

'Don't be absurd, Amelia, you do not even

170

know him.'

'I have heard the most unpleasant things about him – that he is cruel to animals and horrible with servants.'

'You should not listen to idle gossip. People always take pleasure in making up slanderous tales.'

'But he *looks* cruel. He has a cruel mouth and eyes – and if he is unkind to animals and servants then who is to say he would not treat a wife just as badly? Surely, Mama, you would not wish me to be married to somebody who might mistreat me?'

'You are talking nonsense, Amelia. None of my enquiries about Lord Henry has led me to suppose any such thing. These are foolish imaginings. Ridiculous excuses, on your part. You will wear your blue silk and you will be amiable to Lord Henry. I shall allow you to go into the garden with him while the countess and I remain indoors to converse, so that you will have the opportunity to make a favourable impression – or as good an impression as you are capable of. I recommend that you talk about the weather – at least you should be able to speak intelligently about *that*.'

'I do not wish to talk with him about

anything, Mama. I have nothing to say to him.'

'That is enough, Amelia! You will do as you are told. And see to it that you do not discourage Lord Henry in the same way that you discouraged Sir John – however that was. He may well be your last chance of securing a husband this Season.'

Amelia said miserably, 'I think I should far sooner die an old maid.'

Mrs Beauclerc drew an impatient breath. She glared at her daughter. 'If you are still entertaining any ridiculous romantic notions about that Captain Young, then you may instantly dismiss them from your mind. I have no intention of allowing you to marry some penniless soldier. Nor has your father. So that is an end of it.'

Lord Henry and his mother were shown in and Amelia seated herself as far away from both as possible. The countess was a frightening-looking woman with cold eyes and a mouth as tight as a closed trap and her son had inherited both features, as well as her large build. In later life, she thought, he would probably become bloated and red-faced. The conversation lurched from one topic to the next – the heat, the dust in the park, the unlikely prospect of rain, the health of the earl and – following Mrs Beauclerc's solicitous enquiry – that of the viscount, who had recently been laid very low, it seemed, with some kind of fever. Amelia observed her mother's struggle to appear suitably dismayed at the news. They then passed on to the overcrowding at the most recent ball. Lord Henry himself contributed little to the flow but Amelia was aware of his eyes frequently looking her over rather as though she were a horse he was considering buying. There was not, she thought with relief, the least affection or admiration in his glances – only a kind of speculation – and so she began to hope that her mother's notion of a serious interest had been quite mistaken.

After they had discussed the ball to death, her mama, with a falsely loving smile bestowed in her direction, instructed her to take Lord Henry into the garden to show him the roses, which, she declared, were at their very best. Mama had scarcely ever actually set foot in the garden and Amelia knew that the roses had suffered in the heat and were well past their best, but she also knew that it was no use arguing. She stood up dutifully and led Lord Henry out by the

French windows.

The faded and drooping roses duly inspected, without comment or interest from his lordship, she began to lead him back towards the house but instead he proposed continuing the walk to the far end of the garden where there was a bench in the shade of a lilac tree. The bench creaked slightly under his weight as he sat down and, again, she sat as far away from him as possible, though this time the distance could be no more than a foot or two. She kept her head turned away but she could feel his eyes upon her, studying her, as before. Presently he spoke.

'Why is it that you never look directly at me, Miss Beauclerc? Is it shyness that prevents you?'

'I was not aware that I didn't, Lord Henry.'

'But you are still keeping your head averted.'

With an effort, she turned it towards him. 'I am sorry. I meant no disrespect.'

'That is better,' he said, nodding. 'I can see your face, which, though it may not be of great beauty is nonetheless pleasing ... as is your figure. I abhor thinness in a woman.' His gaze roamed over her again. 'In fact, I find you altogether pleasing and your timidity has its appeal, I must confess. It adds spice to the proceedings.' When she stayed silent, he went on. 'Let us not pretend. Your mother has high hopes of a betrothal between us and my mother is not averse to the match. Nor, I find, am I – now that I have had the opportunity to consider the matter, and you, further. I assume that you are willing?'

'No, I am not at all willing, Lord Henry – since you ask.'

He stared at her. 'What can you mean?'

'Why, that I do not want to marry you. Not in the very least.' Amelia jumped to her feet. 'I must beg you to excuse me. I should like to return indoors.'

His hand shot out to take hold of her arm. 'One moment, Miss Beauclerc, you are carrying your modesty too far. Be careful lest I take you seriously.'

'Indeed, I assure you that I am perfectly serious. I have no desire to be your wife.'

His eyes narrowed and his grip tightened. 'Is this some game you are playing? Why else have we been despatched to the garden? Why else did you accompany me with such alacrity? I warn you that I do not like to be trifled with, Miss Beauclerc. I am not a patient man.'

She thought of the tales she had heard about him flogging his horses and whipping his dogs and ill-treating his servants and was suddenly very frightened. Fear lent her the strength to wrench free of his grasp and to hurry back towards the house. His fingers had left red weals on her arm.

'What am I to do, Lottie? It seems that Lord Henry is not so easily put off. He is not at all concerned that I have told him that I do not wish to marry him. I do not think he believed me to be in earnest. He has called several times since and Mama talks of nothing but a wedding. What is to be done?' Amelia, seated beside Charlotte at the next ball of the Season, was close to despair.

'When he proposes you must refuse him in no uncertain terms.'

'But he still may not believe me. And Mama will insist that I accept. It is *very* hard to stand up to her.'

'I'm sure that is true, but you must do so. You cannot spend the rest of your life shackled to somebody that you dislike so much. And I have heard nothing good of Lord

Henry, I am bound to say.'

'Nor I.' Amelia turned to her friend in anguish. 'All that I hear is bad. He is a very cruel man. When you refused Lord Nicholas – which I am sorry that you did – did he believe you? Do gentlemen never accept a refusal but must always believe it to be false modesty, or some such strange thing?'

Charlotte coloured a little. 'They may find it difficult – I think that is true – if they are sufficiently conceited in the first place, like Lord Nicholas. But you must hold fast.'

'Then I hope for your sake that you are holding fast where Lord Nicholas is concerned,' Amelia remarked. 'Because I can see him approaching us at this very moment.'

Charlotte greeted him without betraying any of the inner disturbance she felt at meeting with him again. But Lady Fairfax's words kept crossing her mind as she responded politely to his enquiries after her health and well-being, and while he paid similar attention to Amelia. *Gentle, sweet, generous ...* Could this really be true of the shameless reprobate who stood before her? Another of the redeeming features listed so artlessly by Lady Fairfax came unbidden into her thoughts and brought fresh colour to her cheeks which she prayed he would not notice. Presently, Amelia was summoned by her mama to return to her side and she found herself left alone with him.

He said pleasantly: 'I can tell by your demeanor, Lottie, that you are in dread of my resuming my unwelcome advances. You are quite safe from me here, I promise you, and so there is no reason why we may not enjoy a dance. I hope I may have that pleasure?'

She danced a quadrille with him and it was hard not to enjoy the dance with such an accomplished partner. Afterwards he left her with a graceful bow and without demur – indeed, rather too promptly for her taste. She wondered whether he had, in fact, abandoned the scheme for inheriting Maplethorpe and resigned himself to losing it. It would be a pity, she thought, if she were denied the satisfaction of rejecting him again.

Mrs Beauclerc, finding Mr Beauclerc absent from his duties, had run him to earth behind a potted palm in an adjoining room. He was fast asleep in a comfortable armchair and she roused him with a vigorous and indignant shake of his shoulder.

'What can you be thinking of, Roland? I cannot keep watch for every minute by myself.'

He said grumpily: 'Why should that be necessary? The ball can surely proceed perfectly well to its conclusion without our constant supervision.'

She snorted. 'It is your daughter who requires the supervision. I dare not take my eyes off her for fear that Captain Young, or some other equally unsuitable young man, attempts to ingratiate himself with her. You know very well how susceptible she is – without a shred of common sense. And with Lord Henry so close to making his proposal, I do not intend that anything, or anyone, shall stand in his way.'

'How do you know that he is close to any such thing?'

'Why he and the countess have called on us twice in the past week and he has been paying the most marked attention to Amelia. There is no doubt that he means to offer for her before the Season is out – thank heavens. He is not *entirely* all that I wished for her – the elder brother would have been preferable – but he will do quite well.'

'Is Amelia of the same opinion, I wonder?'

'Her opinion is of no consequence. She is too young to have such a thing and, if she were to, then it would be bound to be a very foolish one.'

'I should not like her to be wed to somebody she did not care for.'

'She scarcely knows him, as I have pointed out to her, which is all to the good. I think it a great mistake to know one's future husband too well before marriage.'

'Or one's future wife,' he muttered grimly. He yawned and rose unwillingly to his feet, wincing at the pain thereby caused. Accompanying Mrs Beauclerc to her lookout post in the ballroom, he submitted himself to at least two more hours of excruciating boredom and discomfort.

Thirteen

Mrs Beauclerc's prediction proved correct. To Amelia's dismay, Lord Henry, quite undeterred by her coldness towards him – in fact, if anything, goaded by it – asked permission of her father to address her. Permission was granted, to her even greater distress, though she inferred from overhearing part of a later loud exchange in the study between her parents that it had been given reluctantly. 'Don't care for the fellow,' Papa had avowed. 'Something damned unsavoury about him, if you ask me.' Mama, of course, had replied that she was *not* asking him and that they were very fortunate that a gentleman of Lord Henry's birth and breeding had offered at the last ditch, else they would have found themselves with all the awkwardness of an unmarried daughter on their hands, having to make do eventually with somebody of far less consequence. And there was always the chance, Mama, had further declared optimistically, of Lord Henry's elder brother, the heir to the earldom, succumbing to some fatal illness or breaking his neck in the hunting field.

Accordingly, Lord Henry presented himself the following day and Amelia was told to receive him in the withdrawing room.

'Naturally, you will accept him,' Mama instructed. 'And do so with both modesty and grace. I do not wish Lord Henry to be put off at the last moment by any of your unfortunate gaucheness.'

When she entered the room Lord Henry was standing by the fireplace. At least he was not admiring his reflection, as Lord Pomeroy had done, but then, Amelia said to herself, there would have been nothing whatever to admire. She looked at his coarse face and heavy figure with fear and dread and she fancied that he was perfectly aware of her fear – and that far from annoying, it pleased him. She remained standing behind the sofa so that it stood like a bulwark between the two of them. He bowed and addressed her without preamble.

'Miss Beauclerc, as you are no doubt aware your father has given his permission for me to speak to you. As you are no doubt also aware, your mother has accorded her full support. When last the subject of marriage was raised between us, you declared yourself to be unwilling. I took your response for some kind of ploy – a game that you were playing with me for some private reasons of your own – and I confess that it only intrigued me the more. The chase is far more exciting, I find, when the quarry is elusive. In short, you made me all the more determined by your apparent reluctance for I never care to be thwarted. A clever trick indeed. I am here, after all, to ask you to accept my proposal and to become my wife.'

She found that she had begun to shake like a leaf. The prospect of marriage to this man, raking her with his cold eyes, was so horrible that it was a moment before she found her voice. When she did it sounded breathless and squeaky and not at all firm as she intended. 'I thank you for your proposal and the honour that you do me, Lord Henry, but I regret that I cannot accept. It was not any ploy on my part, as you imagined. I was not playing any game. I sincerely meant what I said. I do not wish to marry you, and there's an end to it.'

'Am I really supposed to believe that?'

'You may believe it, or not, as you please,' she said, gripping the back of the sofa to give herself courage. 'It is the truth.'

He flushed a deep, angry red. 'Have a care, Miss Beauclerc, lest I lose patience with you completely. I warned you, I am not a man to be thwarted. My own parents are not averse to the match and your parents have given their full consent. It is your duty to obey their wishes. To remember your duty to them. Obedience is a prime virtue in any woman. Surely they taught you that?' Seeing that she did not know what to reply, he took a step forward and smiled now – a smile without warmth or affection: a smile of triumph. 'So, we may inform them of the happy news, may we not? We are betrothed and shall be married as soon as it can be arranged. I must confess to some impatience...'

He took more steps and she retreated before him, backing towards the door. 'I beg that you will not inform them of any such thing, Lord Henry. We are *not* betrothed and never will be. *Never.*' She seized the door handle behind her and wrenched at it. Mama was close by in the hall, all ears, and started to speak to her. She paid no heed but ran past her and on up the stairs, pell-mell, until she reached the sanctity of her bedroom.

'Open this door at once, Amelia.' Mama's voice sounded terrifying in its fury and the handle rattled violently. *'At once.'*

A half-hour or more had passed since the interview with Lord Henry which Amelia had spent crouched on her knees beside her bed with her fingers stuffed in her ears. She had no idea what had passed downstairs after she had taken flight, nor did she know whether Lord Henry had left the house or was, perhaps, still present. She rose slowly to her feet. 'Has he gone?'

'I assume you mean Lord Henry,' Mama snapped. 'Of course he has gone and is not likely to return without a full apology from you.' The handle rattled again. 'Open the door or I shall fetch someone to break it down.'

'I am not going to marry him, if that's what you want.'

'You will be fortunate indeed if he still wishes to marry *you* after you insulted him in such a manner.' Rattle, rattle went the door handle, more violently than ever. 'Open the door this minute.'

She turned the key reluctantly and the door burst open. Mama entered the room and stood with hands on her hips, glaring. 'Well, what have you to say for yourself?'

'Only that I will not marry Lord Henry.'

'Indeed you *will*. After all the time – and money – that has been spent on securing you a suitable husband your father and I do not intend to allow you to turn down such an opportunity. I have succeeded in persuading Lord Henry that it is only nervousness that led you to behave in such a foolish and wild manner. Fortunately, he has accepted that explanation and is prepared to overlook what occurred. It is extremely generous of him.'

'He is not generous at all. He is horrible and I hate him.' Amelia began to weep. 'Please, Mama, do not try to force me to marry him for I should be most miserably unhappy.'

Mrs Beauclerc snorted. 'Happiness has nothing to do with marriage, and the sooner you learn that the better. Marriage is about one's station in society, about enjoying the respect and comfort that is one's due. The most that one may hope for, otherwise, is a reasonable degree of contentment. To wish for more is nothing but sheer folly. Your infatuation with that useless Army captain has led you to take leave of your senses, Amelia. You will stay in this room on bread and water until you return to them.' She removed the key from the inside of the door. 'And until you apologize to Lord Henry and humbly accept his proposal.'

The door slammed shut and the key turned. Amelia put her hands over her face and wept in earnest.

'Begging your pardon, miss, but this is for you.'

Charlotte, returning from a short stroll in search of some fresh outdoor air, was startled by the waif-like girl who accosted her near the front door. She looked at the letter thrust under her nose and saw her name written there. The writing – resembling a drunken spider crawling across the envelope – she recognized immediately as Amelia's. She also recognized the girl as one of the parlour maids belonging to the Beauclerc household. A timid soul who scuttled about like a little mouse.

'It's Kitty, isn't it?' she said, wondering why on earth Amelia had used her to deliver the missive.

She bobbed a curtsey. 'Yes, miss. Miss Amelia told me to give this to you. Into your hands alone, she said. Nobody else's. And I was to tell you that it's very urgent.'

Charlotte took the letter, frowning. 'Is something wrong, Kitty? Has something happened?'

The parlour maid's face crumpled in distress. 'Oh, yes, miss. They've gone and locked poor Miss Amelia in her bedroom and she's not to come out until she agrees to marry Lord Henry Vane. Bread and water is all she's had to eat these past two days. I've taken it up to her myself on a tray ... that's when she gave me the letter. Slipped it into my apron pocket, see, and told me to be sure take it to you here at this address as quickly as I could. And I was to bring back a reply from you.'

Charlotte touched her shoulder. 'Thank you, Kitty. You've done very well. Just wait here for a little while and I will give you a reply to take back.' She took the letter indoors and sat down to read it. It was stained by many tears.

Dearest Charlotte,

I am in such trouble – you cannot imagine! Lord Henry proposed to me and when I refused him Mama was so angry that she locked me up in my bedroom on bread and water. She says that I am to stay here until I agree to marry him and, as I shall never do that, I shall probably starve to death. She has told Papa that I am being wilfully disobedient and must be taught a lesson. Kitty (our parlour maid) says that Papa has shut himself up in the library and washed his hands of everything so there is no help to be had there.

You are the only one that I can turn to, dearest Charlotte. You know how dreadfully unhappy I should be to have to marry Lord Henry. He is the most horrid person I know and I should sooner kill myself. Will you go to see Captain Young and tell him what has happened? If he truly loves me, as I love him – and I am quite certain that he does – then he will somehow rescue me. We could elope together – flee to Gretna Green where we could be married. Once that has happened then there is nothing that Mama could do to make me marry Lord Henry and I should be the happiest of creatures on this earth instead of the most miserable.

Please send word at once. Kitty will bring a letter to me secretly. She can be trusted.

Your loving friend,
Amelia.

She sat down at her writing bureau and took up a quill.

Fourteen

Captain Young was very surprised to receive a visit from Miss Craven. Conscious of the lack of any great comfort or elegance in his bachelor lodgings in Smith Street, he did his best to improve matters – offering her the best chair and dusting it over quickly with a handkerchief. She declined the seat, however, remaining standing and with such a worried expression that he asked at once what was the matter?

'It is Amelia,' she told him. 'And I do not know what to do about it all.' She went on to show him the tear-stained letter that she had received. His face darkened as he read it. He looked up.

'Surely Mrs Beauclerc cannot mean to force her daughter into a marriage so repugnant to her?'

'Well, she cannot, of course, actually physically drag her to the altar, but I am very much afraid that, with time, Amelia may give way. She has always found it very hard to stand up to her mama. Mrs Beauclerc is, as you have no doubt already discovered, exceedingly forceful and determined.'

The captain remembered Nicholas's dry description of the lady as a prize sow guarding its only piglet. At the time it had amused him, but this was no longer a laughing matter. He said gravely, 'As to my own feelings, Miss Craven, they are as constant and true as Miss Beauclerc believes, but some time ago I had reached the conclusion that I had no right to lay any claim to her heart and hand when she could marry to so much better advantage.' He gestured round the room. 'As you see, I have very little to offer, except for myself. To take advantage of her unhappy situation by such a rash step as elopement, bringing her reputation into disrepute, would be the action of an unprincipled man.'

She nodded. 'I guessed that you would think so and I am glad to hear you speak thus, but I beg you to consider that it is Amelia's whole future happiness that is at stake. By all accounts that I have heard, Lord Henry Vane is a cruel and heartless man.

Her life with him would be wretched. Her feelings for you, though, are as true as your own for her and she would gladly risk everything for your sake.' She met his eyes frankly. 'I came here not only to show you her letter but also to offer my help. I am convinced that we must act and act soon. Somehow we must free Amelia and take her away – not to Gretna Green but to some place where you and she may be married in secret by a priest. I will undertake to chaperone her on the journey until the ceremony can take place, in order that the least amount of damage may be done to her reputation.'

He stared at her. 'You would do that?'

'Certainly. Amelia is my dearest friend and I cannot stand by and see her happiness destroyed. I shall do everything I can to preserve it. But exactly how we are to achieve this, I confess I am at a loss to say...'

Captain Young paced about the room for a moment. 'The room where she is imprisoned is on the first floor?'

'Yes, at the back of the house. The window gives on to the garden and I know which one it is. There is a brick wall surrounding the garden and a gate at the far end which opens on to the mews. If we could find a ladder tall enough to reach the window then Amelia could climb down.'

He said at once. 'No harm must come to her.'

'You can carry her down over your shoulder,' Miss Craven suggested calmly. 'But what happens when we reach that stage I am not quite certain. How are we to make our escape? Amelia, I have to say, is not a very accomplished horsewomen. It will have to be in some kind of carriage, not on horse-back, though where we are to lay hands on one I haven't a notion.'

'I have,' he said, ceasing his pacing and turning to face her. 'Nicholas has one.'

'I'd sooner ask for help from almost any-body else in London.'

'I am sorry, indeed, that you feel that way towards him,' he told her. 'But for the sake of Miss Beauclerc's happiness, your scruples could perhaps be put aside?'

She nodded. 'You are quite right. Though a curricle would be of no use for such a journey with us all.'

'He has another carriage that will serve the purpose very well. A landau.'

'Did he also win it at the tables?'

The captain smiled at her tart rejoinder.

'Not to my knowledge. He is a first-rate whip, you know, and I'll wager that he would be willing to take the reins himself. In which case no one will catch us.'

She was silent for a moment. 'I cannot allow my aversion to Lord Nicholas to stand in the way of rescuing my dear friend. Ask him, if you will, Captain Young, but I implore you to bind him to the utmost secrecy.'

'I promise you that he can be the very soul of discretion, when he chooses.'

'I can believe that of him, at least,' she said.

'What do you say, Nicholas? Will you help?'

'Naturally I will, Clive. It will give me considerable pleasure to thwart Mrs Beauclerc's misplaced ambitions. Miss Beauclerc is far too nice to be saddled with such an odious fellow as Henry Vane. I have no doubt whatever that you will make her an infinitely better husband. You have my complete support. Just tell me where and when the elopement is to take place.'

'It is not yet arranged precisely. Word has to be taken secretly to Miss Beauclerc and a time fixed. Details to be planned.'

'Do stop pacing about like a lion in a cage. It's simple enough.'

'What is *not* so simple is what happens after we release her, Nicholas. Miss Craven has been good enough to say that she will accompany Miss Beauclerc as chaperone until she and I can be married. But where we are to go and what priest can be prevailed on to marry us in these circumstances is not so certain. To go all the way to Gretna Green is a poor notion – Miss Craven and I are both agreed on that.'

Lord Nicholas studied the glass of brandy in his hand. 'Lottie is nothing if not practical. What other suggestion has she offered then?'

'None. And I'm blessed if I know what to do either. Once it is discovered that Miss Beauclerc is missing then there'll be a hue and cry after us.'

'To have Mrs Beauclerc in hot pursuit after one is not a happy prospect, I agree. Infinitely worse than a pack of hounds.'

'Be serious, for God's sake, Nicholas. What the devil am I to do for the best?'

'First arrange the rescue hour with Miss Beauclerc through the maid, Kitty – an hour before dawn, I advise, so that the escape can be made under cover of darkness and there is time to put some distance between yourself and your pursuers before daylight. It will take approximately two days to reach Maplethorpe.'

'*Maplethorpe?* But what about your aunt? Would she welcome us?'

'Aunt Augusta is safely here in London and likely to remain until the end of the Season. There will be no difficulty in our taking refuge there. It's my second home.'

'You will accompany us, then?'

'Naturally. You wish to travel at speed, I take it? I shall drive the two ladies in the carriage while you ride escort.' Lord Nicholas paused to drink some brandy. 'As for the small problem of finding a priest willing to marry you – the parson there owes his living to Aunt Augusta and the family. I think you will find that he will be eager to oblige in that respect. And there is a private chapel in the house so that the ceremony can take place quite unobserved.'

Captain Young sank down in the armchair opposite. 'Good God, Nicholas, one would have said that you'd done all this yourself before.'

'Oh, I had something of the sort in mind years ago, as a matter of fact, when I was much younger and very green. There was an older woman for whom I had conceived a great fancy. I was quite out of my mind over her. In thrall, you might say. Fortunately, I discovered in the nick of time that she already had a husband else I might have been involved in some tiresome duel. Since then I have not been tempted to repeat the performance.'

'Not even with Miss Craven?'

The other gazed into his glass. 'Much as I might relish the idea of an elopement with Lottie, I fear she would not entertain for one moment the idea of eloping with me.'

'Well, she did say that she would sooner ask for help from almost anyone else in London.'

'Did she indeed?'

'But that she could not allow her aversion for you to stand in her way of rescuing Miss Beauclerc.'

'A great sacrifice on her part.'

Captain Young looked regretfully at his friend. 'She dislikes you exceedingly, I'm afraid, Nicholas. There seems little chance of your changing her mind on that score. I'm very sorry. It means, of course, that you will lose Maplethorpe, but, apart from that consideration, lately I have somehow felt you were well suited to each other.'

Lord Nicholas smiled. 'Do you know, Clive, lately I have somehow felt exactly the same.'

Charlotte lay awake for most of the night listening to the clock on the landing outside her bedroom chiming the hours and the quarters. She was well aware of the opprobrium that would descend on her head when her part in the elopement was discovered. There was bound to be a scandal and Mama and Papa were certain to be exceedingly vexed and upset – as they would have every right to be – but she could not let that stop her from helping Amelia, any more than she could allow Lord Nicholas's involvement to stop her either. Her own feelings were unimportant. Amelia must be rescued from a miserable future with the odious Lord Henry Vane.

The clock struck three and then a quarter past; at half past the hour she rose and dressed quickly. The letter for Mama had already been written and sealed the night before. Pausing only to put on her bonnet and cape and to pick up the small portmanteau that she had packed, she let herself out of her bedroom and tiptoed down the stairs to the hall. The servants would not be stirring for another two hours and the household was completely silent. She left the letter on the silver tray on the hall table where Clutterbuck would find it and opened the front door quietly. Outside it was still dark, the night air cool and fresh, but the first faint glimmerings of light were already showing above the rooftops towards the east.

The house that the Beauclercs had taken for the Season was only two streets away and Captain Young was waiting in the mews alley at the back, dismounted from his horse and with a ladder ready. They conferred in whispers. Lord Nicholas was bringing the carriage, he assured her in answer to her anxious enquiry. To do so earlier might have roused attention. 'We may count on him, Miss Craven.'

She had grave doubts that they could do anything of the kind but there was nothing for it but to carry on with the plan. By pre-arrangement, Kitty had concealed the key to the garden door in the wall under a stone in the alley and they opened it and, between them, carried the ladder through and across the lawn towards the back of the house. In the pale light of dawn, Amelia could be seen at the sash window, leaning over the sill and waving. The captain set the ladder against the wall and climbed up to bring down first a portmanteau, which, by the way he struggled with it, looked to be exceedingly full, and then assist Amelia herself. Wisely, given his beloved's equally awkward weight, he guided her down tenderly, rung by rung, rather than attempting to carry her. Once they had safely reached the bottom, there was no time to be lost. The ladder was returned against its hayloft in the stables nearby and scarcely had that been achieved than there came the sharp clip-clop of hooves and a hooded carriage entered the mews alley, wheeling fast over the cobblestones. The tall figure of its driver was unmistakable to Charlotte, as was the big, shaggy dog trotting alongside. The horses were brought to a pawing halt, the two portmanteaus stowed away and she and Amelia were handed up, with only the briefest of exchanges. Captain Young had leaped upon his horse and in a twinkling of an eye they were off, swinging out of the alley on to the main street and heading west away from the dawn.

Mrs Beauclerc burst into the library like an enraged bull charging into a bullring. Her husband, who had been enjoying a peaceful and contemplative moment, a volume of learned philosophical essays open on his knee and his spectacles on his nose – for the sake of appearances – came to with a start. His wife flung her arms wide.

'She has gone! Run off! I shall never forgive her. Never! The ingratitude! The disobedience! The shame! The *scandal*!'

Her husband sighed. 'Calm yourself, Dorothea. What is all this to-do? Who has gone off?'

'Why Amelia, of course. Who else should I be speaking of? She escaped out of her bedroom window?'

'How could she? It's more than fifteen feet to the ground.'

'How should I know? A ladder? A rope? By whatever deceitful means she was able to contrive. Of course, she could not have done it alone. She was aided and abetted by that worthless man.'

'What worthless man?'

'Captain Young, who else? That penniless creature who has been trying to worm his way into her affections all Season. It is he who is responsible for all this. She has run off with him. Eloped! They must be stopped. He must be arrested and court-martialled. Thrown into prison. Disgraced for ever.'

Mr Beauclerc took off his spectacles and polished them carefully with his handkerchief. 'So far as I am aware, elopement is not a court-martial offence.'

'Of course it is! It is conduct unfitting to an officer and a gentleman. He will pay dearly for his impudence. How *can* you sit here calmly reading, Roland, when such a dreadful thing has happened?'

'Until this moment I was not aware that anything at all had happened,' he pointed out drily.

'Lord Henry will never marry her now. There is no hope of it. None whatever.'

'Apparently not, since she appears to be on the brink of marrying someone else. Which seems to me rather a blessing. I never much cared for the prospect of having that fellow as a son-in-law. If you had not been so set on the idea, I should have turned him down flat. In my opinion, she showed good sense when *she* did – for the second time in her life.'

'*Good sense*! Wilful stupidity, more like. A

marriage to Lord Henry Vane would have allied us to one of the noblest families in the country. A title! The possibility of the earldom, even! By all acounts the elder brother is *not* in robust health.' Mrs Beauclerc wrung her hands. 'I cannot bear to think of what she has thrown away. And all for the sake of a foolish infatuation for a nobody.'

Mr Beauclerc closed the book of essays with a sigh and placed it on the table beside him. 'How can you be so certain that Captain Young has anything to do with this affair?'

'Because she left a letter, of course. Addressed to us.'

'And what did she say?'

'That she is going to marry him and that Charlotte Craven is to act as chaperone until such time as the ceremony takes place.'

'At least you may comfort yourself with that. Miss Craven has always struck me as eminently reliable.'

'*Reliable!* To aid and abet such madness? She has been grossly disloyal to us to plot with Amelia when I have always been most civil to her. We must go after them at once, Roland.' Mrs Beauclerc seized her husband by the arm and attempted to drag him to his feet. 'Put a stop to it all.'

He removed her hand firmly. 'Just one thing, my dear. In which direction are we to go?'

'You may open the window, Snettisham. But only a small amount. I won't have draughts blowing down my neck.'

Miss Snettisham, who had been feeling quite faint from the heat and stuffiness of the room, rose thankfully to wrestle with the sash window. It was almost beyond her strength to move it at all, so seldom was it opened and so firmly stuck, but she managed to tug it up a few inches at the bottom and breathed in outside air which seemed almost as hot as that inside. She had regained her customary seat in the corner and picked up her needlework when the butler, Mason, announced Lady Craven, who entered the room apparently in a state of great nervous distress.

'Oh, Augusta, something most terrible has happened!' Her ladyship collapsed into a chair, eyes closed and fanned herself with her hand. 'You cannot imagine how distraught I am.'

'I do not have to imagine it,' Lady Fairfax

responded briskly. 'I can see for myself. Fetch the salts quickly, Snettisham.'

Miss Snettisham scurried to do her employer's bidding and wafted the phial of sal volatile to and fro under Lady Craven's nostrils. After a moment her ladyship's eyes flickered open and she gave a moan. 'Thomas will be appalled when he learns of it. How could Charlotte be party to such a thing! How *could* she?'

'I am quite unable to answer the question when I have no notion what she has done,' Lady Fairfax remarked. 'Compose yourself, Sophia, and tell me what has happened that is so very terrible?'

Lady Craven waved away the smelling salts. 'Amelia Beauclerc has eloped with Captain Young and Charlotte is accompanying them to act as chaperone until they can be married. Clutterbuck found a letter for me on the hall table this morning. She must have gone secretly during the night.'

Lady Fairfax grunted. 'What on earth inspired her to take such a drastic course of action?'

'It seems that Mrs Beauclerc had locked her daughter in her room until she consented to marry Lord Henry Vane whom she does not wish to marry in the least.'

'Nor should I. Henry Vane is most dis-agreeable. So is his mother. Captain Young is greatly to be preferred.'

'Not by Mrs Beauclerc, I understand.'

'That does not surprise me. The captain has neither title nor fortune, though he has a great deal else to offer, but she would never have the wit to see it. It seems to me, Sophia, that you are making a great deal of fuss over nothing. Miss Beauclerc will doubtless marry Captain Young and Charlotte's presence with her up until the moment when they are man and wife will ensure the minimum of scandal and gossip. There is bound to be some but it will soon blow over and be forgotten.'

Some colour returned to Lady Craven's cheeks and she sat up straighter. 'Do you really think so, Augusta?'

'Certainly. Charlotte's part in the affair may be somewhat rash but I have no doubt that she acted from the best of motives – concern for her friend's happiness. There is no disgrace in that. The only disgrace, in my opinion, lies with Mrs Beauclerc for having tried to force her daughter to marry Henry Vane. Abominable woman!'

It passed through Lady Craven's mind that Augusta Fairfax was by no means above trying to force people to marry people they did not wish to, but she forbore to comment. 'Where could they have gone to, I wonder? Charlotte did not say. Gretna Green, do you think?'

'Too far. I would guess rather closer.' Lady Fairfax frowned. 'Do you know by what means they are travelling?'

'I have no idea. They cannot all get on to one horse. By stage coach, I suppose. Captain Young has no carriage of his own so I cannot think of another way.'

'I can.'

Lady Craven stared. 'What do you mean?'

'My nephew, Nicholas, is a good friend of Captain Young, in case you had forgotten. I think it very probable that he has lent his landau for the purpose. And also quite likely that he is driving it himself. An escapade of that kind would be very much to his taste.'

Lady Craven put up her hand to her eyes and gave another moan. 'If that is so and *he* is with them, then Charlotte's reputation is lost. The story will be all round London.'

'Fetch the salts again quickly, Snettisham.' Lady Fairfax waited while they were administered and Lady Craven's moans turned to chokes. 'That's enough. You're asphyxiating her.' She rapped her cane on the floor. 'Now, Sophia, there is no cause for all this panic and hysteria. Charlotte's reputation will be perfectly safe. Kindly remember that she is going to marry Nicholas in any case.'

'I would remind *you*, Augusta, that she has refused him.'

Lady Fairfax waved a hand dismissively. 'She'll have him in the end, mark my words. It's only a question of time. Her turning him down intrigued him. He's *determined* to have her now. She won't be able be able to hold out for ever. Not against Nicholas.'

Lady Craven rather wondered if she herself would; Miss Snettisham who had retired once more to her unobtrusive corner seat and her needlework was very certain that *she* would not. The whole tale had sounded wonderfully romantic to her and she envied Miss Craven with all her heart.

'If only we knew *where* they were going, Augusta. It could be anywhere in the whole of England – or Scotland, if they do decide to go to Gretna Green.'

'I told you, it will not be Gretna Green.'

'How can you be so sure?'

'Because I know Nicholas. If he *is* involved, he will almost certainly take them to Maplethorpe. A far more practical plan. The parson there will marry Captain Young and Miss Beauclerc in the private chapel.'

'He might refuse.'

'Indeed he will not.'

'How do you know?'

'Because Mr Trimble does what he's told. The living belongs to Maplethorpe and the family.'

Lady Craven struggled to her feet. She said with dignity. 'In that case, I must leave for Maplethorpe at once. Whatever you say, Augusta, I cannot leave Charlotte in the clutches of your disreputable nephew. You know very well how he is. Anything might happen. *Anything!*'

'If you are going to keep gasping in that ridiculous way, Snettisham, kindly leave the room.' Lady Fairfax banged her cane loudly again. '*Sit down*, Sophia, and use your head for once.'

Lady Craven did so unwillingly. 'Well, I must do *something*.'

'Not yet. We shall, indeed, leave for Maplethorpe – you and I – but not yet. If we reach there too soon and interrupt them, we may prevent the very thing occurring that we both hope for.'

Sophia Craven looked aghast. 'Surely you are not suggesting...'

'Of course not. Don't be absurd! I merely meant that we must give Nicholas time to win Charlotte over. A day, two days perhaps. I guarantee it won't take much longer. Don't forget they will be at Maplethorpe, which has charms of its own. Charlotte will find it very hard to resist both Nicholas *and* Maplethorpe.' Lady Fairfax gave a slow and satisfied smile. 'Pull the bell, Snettisham. Lady Craven and I will take some lime cordial. You may have some too. It might stop you making those peculiar noises all the time.'

Fifteen

The journey to Maplethorpe was accomplished in two days with an overnight stop at the King's Arms inn, where it was clear that Lord Nicholas was well known. Every courtesy and assistance was offered, the best rooms made instantly available and an exceedingly good meal served in a private parlour. Retiring for the night in the comfortable bedroom which she shared with Amelia, Charlotte had to admit that Lord Nicholas had conducted himself, so far, in a faultless manner, behaving with the utmost propriety. She had expected nothing less from Captain Young, who rode escort alongside the carriage, and the care and concern that he showed for Amelia at every opportunity persuaded her that right had been done. Amelia herself was bubbling over with happiness and relief to have escaped her prison and a dreadful fate.

'It would have been far worse than death,' she declared. 'I should have taken poison rather than endure intimacy with such a man. Oh, Charlotte, I am so grateful to you for helping Captain Young to rescue me. I hope you will not be in too much trouble with your mama. For myself, I find I no longer care what *my* mama says. When next I see her, Captain Young and I will be married and she may be as angry as she likes. She will not be able to undo what has been done.'

Charlotte, who could imagine Mrs Beauclerc's wrath only too well, had been comforting herself with the thought that Amelia's mama could not possibly know their route or their destination and that they had travelled at such a speed that any pursuit must surely be far behind. So long as the marriage ceremony took place immediately, all should be well.

They reached Maplethorpe late on the second day. The house lay in a gentle dip in the land, protected from wind and weather and encircled by a ring of great trees – beech and oak and ash and sycamore – and parkland with grazing deer. The evening sunlight bathed its old stone walls and mullioned windows with a soft, golden glow and cast long, purple shadows across the lawns. Since her last visit, years ago as a child, Charlotte had forgotten, or perhaps never quite appreciated, what a beautiful place it was. How peaceful and unspoiled. How mellow and warm and welcoming. She could understand quite well how much someone might wish to keep such an inheritance, but it was more difficult to comprehend how Lord Nicholas, with his evident taste for a fast London life and all its diversions, could care so much about somewhere so quiet and tranquil. Perhaps there was, indeed, another side to him that she had never seen?

He handed her down from the carriage. 'Welcome to Maplethorpe, Charlotte. I shall endeavour to make it a more pleasant experience for you this time.'

Inside, the house matched its exterior. All was as it should be: soft-coloured furnishings in a country style with none of the modish extravagances of London. Nothing, she suspected, had been altered for years. If I had been mistress here, she thought, I should not have changed anything either. I should have left it just exactly as it is.

The wedding ceremony in the family

chapel had been proposed for the following morning, when they were rested from the journey, but, to Charlotte's dismay, the servant who had been sent to fetch the parson from his house soon after their arrival returned with the news that the Reverend Trimble was absent, visiting his sick mother in the neighbouring county, and was not expected back until two days hence.

Amelia, hearing the news, went pale and began to tremble. *'Two days!* Mama will surely find us in that time. She will be bound to discover where we are. She will come here and force me to return to London.'

Charlotte tried to calm her but was, inwardly, equally uneasy. It was very possible that Lord Nicholas's carriage had been observed in the mews at that early hour and identified. Mrs Beauclerc, if she was not already well aware of it, would have been informed of Captain Young's friendship with Lord Nicholas. Two and two could very quickly make four. And four was Maplethorpe. The next morning she rose early and went in search of Lord Nicholas. She found him out in the stable yard, talking to one of the grooms with Marmaduke sitting quietly at his heels. He was dressed in plain country riding clothes which became him quite as much, she noted objectively, as his fashionable town attire. When she spoke to him of Amelia's fears, and of her own, he reassured her. A groom had been dispatched on horseback with a letter for the priest, instructing him to return immediately.

'He will be here by tomorrow and will conduct the ceremony forthwith.' Lord Nicholas smiled at her. 'If necessary in his riding boots. Meantime, since it is a beautiful morning, I propose that we go riding ourselves. Come and see the horses and pick one for yourself.'

'But I have no suitable clothes.'

'There are plenty here,' he told her. 'Habits belonging to my aunt when she was a girl and probably those from her mother and grandmother too. All carefully kept. You have only to go and choose one – after you have chosen your mount.'

The stable block, with its tall clock tower and cobbled yard, was well-kept – swept spotlessly clean, the stalls and loose boxes all with fresh straw and water. She went with him from one horse to another, stroking their noses, admiring, considering. The choice was hard but, in the end, she settled on a bay, sixteen hands at least, she judged, and with a spirited look about him.

'The grey mare, Verity, might suit you better,' Lord Nicholas demurred. 'A much quieter ride than Vulcan.'

She saw that he assumed her to be accustomed to docile hacks bred and broken for ladies to venture out on at a sedate pace. 'You said I could choose,' she reminded him.

'I thought that you would choose more wisely.'

'He looks very fine.'

'He is, but he's hard to control. I usually ride him myself.'

'Then perhaps you could ride the grey mare instead?'

She was shown at least a dozen riding habits by Lady Fairfax's maid who laid them out on the bed before her. Some of them, she saw by their style belonged to days and fashions of long ago but, amongst them, she found one made of dark green barathea with silk frogging to fasten the close-fitting jacket, a sweeping skirt long enough for her height, and a tricorn hat to match. 'It suits you much better than a ball gown,' Amelia told her frankly. 'I have never seen you look so elegant.'

Lord Nicholas was waiting with a groom and two horses – Vulcan and another. Not the quiet grey mare for himself, she noted, but a beautiful chestnut. He watched her approach.

'I wish you had chosen your horse as well as you have chosen your habit, Lottie,' he said grimly. 'I'd far sooner you rode Verity. Or at least take this chesnut. She has perfect manners.'

'Oh, no, I insist on Vulcan,' she insisted stubbornly. 'I like him much the best.'

His obvious disapproval and disquiet induced a spirit of mischief in Charlotte. For all he knew from that awkward ride home on his horse when she had hurt her ankle, she was an indifferent horsewoman. She pretended to be very clumsy mounting the animal, as though she scarcely knew how, and sat on the saddle, clinging tight to the reins with one hand and clutching at Vulcan's mane with the other. He began to plunge around and she let herself flop about like a ragdoll as if she might fall off at any moment. Lord Nicholas leaned from his mount and grasped at her reins. 'This won't do at all, Lottie. I cannot allow it. You must dismount and take this one instead.' He gave a curt order to the groom standing by and dismounted himself. As he did so he let go of the reins for a moment and Charlotte, with a surreptitious kick to Vulcan's flank, clattered off wildly across the yard and out under the archway. Another kick and she was away, cantering fast over the parkland. At first she carried on with the pretence of being a shockingly bad rider, lurching this way and that. But when she heard the thud of hooves behind her and realized that Lord Nicholas was gaining on her, she collected herself and set Vulcan at a full gallop up the long incline of a hill towards a group of trees at the top. She reached them first and reined in the horse who came to an obedient halt. Lord Nicholas rode up on the chestnut, his face white and angry, Marmaduke close behind him. There was a good deal of satisfaction, she thought, in having tricked *him* for a change. She patted Vulcan's neck calmly and called out: 'He goes well enough but not quite as fast as some that I am used to.'

He pulled up beside her. 'My compliments, Charlotte. You certainly fooled me. I had no idea that you were such an accomplished horsewoman.'

'I have ridden since an early age. I believe

I ride rather better than I dance or sew.'

He smiled slightly at that. 'I believe you do. But I beg you to take more care in future, nonethless. You could have been badly hurt.'

His face was still pale and his concern appeared to be genuine but she reminded herself that he was a master at deception. He still imagines that he can win me over, she thought. He would do anything to keep his inheritance. Use any trick or subterfuge.

They rode on up through the trees where sunlight filtered through green leaves and dappled the mossy ground. Apart from birdsong and the soft click of the horses' hooves and Marmaduke's panting, all was quiet. At the far side they emerged on to parkland again, the house below them in the distance. He reined in the chestnut. 'One of the loveliest houses in all England, don't you think?'

'It's very beautiful,' she agreed. 'And it is my understanding that it will be yours one day.'

'How did you learn that?'

'I cannot recall,' she said innocently. 'Mama must have mentioned it, I suppose. It is so, isn't it?'

'I had hoped so,' he replied. 'If it does not come to me, then it will pass to my elder brother, Edwin.' Surely he was not going to admit the whole truth to her? To reveal the despicable deception he had played? But he went on: 'For Maplethorpe's sake I trust that will never happen. My brother has no regard whatever for the place and my sister-in-law, Maria, considers it disgracefully shabby and old-fashioned. She would not be content until she has torn down the west wing and altered all the rest to suit her hideous taste.'

Charlotte thought regretfully again of the sour-featured countess and her proposals for Maplethorpe. She said impulsively, 'How sad that would be. *Nothing* should be changed. It is perfect as it is.'

He turned to her, his face serious. 'Oh, I knew you would think so, Lottie. I knew that you would love it too.'

Be very careful, she warned herself sternly. This is yet another of his ploys.

They rode on down to the house, Marmaduke following them.

'I have heard a most *interesting* piece of news today, Edwin.'

The earl, toying moodily with a slice of tough venison, looked up from his plate. 'What news?'

His countess, when he observed her more closely, appeared flushed purple with excitement. 'It seems that there has been an elopement.'

'An elopement?' he said, disappointed. 'Where's the interest in that?'

'Your brother is involved – there lies the interest,' she said triumphantly.

'You mean he's eloped? *Nicholas?*'

'Not *him*,' she said. 'But the rumour is that he helped a friend of his, a Captain Young, to run off with a Miss Beauclerc. Heiress to a considerable fortune. Lent his carriage for the purpose. Drove it too.'

'Sounds just like Nicholas.'

'Indeed, it does,' she agreed. 'I'm only surprised he didn't elope with Miss Beauclerc and her fortune himself. However, the most interesting part is that, apparently, Miss Craven was prevailed upon to go with them.'

'Miss Craven?'

'For goodness sake, Edwin! Miss Charlotte Craven – the very one that your Aunt Augusta wanted to make Nicholas marry in order to secure his inheritance. Some ridiculous hope that she would reform him – it would take a miracle, nothing less. That Snettleman person, your aunt's companion, let it slip to me – remember?'

'Can't say I do.'

'You never pay proper attention to what I say. The girl refused him, of course. I saw to that.'

'Saw to it?'

'I told you that I would deal with the matter. I informed Miss Craven that Nicholas only wanted to keep Maplethorpe and his inheritance. That it was all a disgraceful trick.'

The earl chewed at the venison, still puzzled. 'Then why did she go with them?'

'As some kind of chaperone, I assume,' the countess said impatiently. 'She is a lifelong friend of Miss Beauclerc's, they say. Of course, her reputation will be equally ruined.'

'How so?'

'Have you lost *all* your wits, Edwin? To be a party to *anything* concerning your brother must inevitably result in ruin. Miss Craven has been travelling unprotected in Nicholas's company. The talk is that they have all fled to Maplethorpe. Imagine what your Aunt Augusta will think of such a use being put to her home! What disgrace and scandal will have been brought upon it! Your brother will have forfeited any possible claim he still has to the place. I think we may safely count on it becoming yours, Edwin. In the fullness of time, of course.'

The earl deposited a piece of half-chewed meat on the side of his plate. 'I wouldn't count on it at all, if I were you.'

'What can you mean?'

He gulped at some wine to wash down the remaining mouthful and wiped his mouth with a napkin. 'You're forgetting that the girl may *have* to marry Nicholas now. Or that Nicholas may have to marry the girl ... Miss Craven, whoever she is. Augusta will make him, if he's compromised her, never mind the inheritance. She's a stickler for that sort of thing. And it's just what she wanted. For all we know, the girl's not too averse to the idea, either, in spite of everything. Most of 'em like him, you know.' He dabbed at his mouth again. 'No, I wouldn't count on anything yet, if I were you, Maria.'

There was a brief silence from the opposite end of the table while the countess reconsidered all the implications. 'We must put a stop to it, Edwin.'

'A stop to what?'

'To any such thing. On no account must

224

Nicholas marry Miss Craven. It must be prevented at all costs.' She rose purposefully from the table. 'Send for the coach. We must leave at once. There is no time to be lost.'

Sixteen

'Tell Samson to go faster, Roland.'

'I've already done so once.'

'Well, it is not fast enough. Tell him again.'

Mr Beauclerc lowered the coach window and leaned forward to put his head out and shout up to the coachman on the box. In the process his hat was knocked sideways and, as the whip was cracked in obedience to his command and the horses plunged forward, he fell backwards heavily on to his wife's lap, dislodging her bonnet as well. When they had disentangled themselves and clothing and seating had been restored to order, he said sourly, 'You'll have us in the ditch, if you're not careful, Dorothea. Then where will we be?'

'Caution must be thrown to the winds,' she declared, 'if we are not to be saddled with a worthless son-in-law.'

The coach lurched on, swinging wildly

from side to side, its occupants flung with it. Mrs Beauclerc held on to her bonnet and Mr Beauclerc his hat and both to the leather straps beside them. As night fell they drew up at an inn. Mrs Beauclerc found fault with everything. The ostlers were slow, the landlord uncivil, the maidservants insolent, the supper uneatable. She summoned the landlord to complain at length about the latter. When she had finally finished she enquired peremptorily if Lord Nicholas Strickland's carriage had called at the inn. The landlord shook his head.

'No, madam.'

'Are you quite *certain*? He must frequently pass this way.'

'I have never, to my knowledge, laid eyes upon the gentleman in question.'

'Or a Captain Young?'

'No, madam. The name means nothing to me.'

'Well, it would mean nothing to most people,' she conceded, dismissing the landlord.

They were retiring for the night – Mrs Beauclerc having rejected two other rooms as unfit for human habitation – when the chambermaid, bearing a jug of hot water, whispered that she had something she could tell … if she was treated right. Mrs Beauclerc glared at her. 'What?'

'She means that if we pay her, she has some information,' her husband said wearily, eyeing the soft feather bed that awaited, so close, after a day's jolting.

'*Pay* her? What impertinence! If you have something to say, girl, say it.'

The chambermaid shook her head. 'Not unless it's worth my while.'

Mrs Beauclerc came to her senses. 'Pay her, Roland.' He tossed over a coin and then, as the chambermaid still hesitated, some more. And then another.

The coins vanished into the chambermaid's apron pocket. 'Lord Nicholas Strickland stayed here last night.'

'Are you sure?'

'Oh yes, ma'am. His lordship often stops here. I saw him with my own eyes.' The girl's pale and plain face glowed suddenly. 'Such a handsome young gentleman. And such lovely manners.'

'We are not interested in either his looks or his manners,' Mrs Beauclerc informed her coldly. 'Was he alone?'

'Oh, no, ma'am. There was two young

ladies with him.' The chambermaid started to giggle and then stopped abruptly as she caught Mrs Beauclerc's eye. 'And another gentleman. A military gentleman. Very nice he was, too. He was on horseback. Lord Nicholas was driving the carriage with the ladies inside. They left early this morning.'

Mrs Beauclerc had drawn a deep breath and now expelled it like a dragon breathing out fire. 'When they departed this morning, which direction did they take?'

'West, ma'am. As I said, his lordship often passes this way, to and from the country.'

When the girl had left the room, Mrs Beauclerc paced up and down in a great fury.

'The landlord lied. Deceived us. How dare he!'

Her husband sat down on the bed, yawning. 'Doubtless he wanted to avoid trouble. That's all.'

'Trouble! I shall give him trouble all right. We leave at daybreak, Roland.' She fixed him with a glare. 'Whether you like it or not.'

In the morning, with fresh horses, the coachman was ordered to resume the fastest pace possible. Mr Beauclerc, dragged from his bed at cockcrow, resigned himself to more hours of acute discomfort. The coach hurtled on down the turnpike, the horses at a gallop. Rounding a bend, a trace broke under the strain and one of the shafts came loose. The coach skewed sideways, turned over and came to rest in a deep ditch.

Lady Fairfax and Lady Craven, with Miss Snettisham squashed uncomfortably between them, were proceeding at a gentler pace in the Fairfax coach, there being no necessity, in Augusta Fairfax's considered opinion, to rush. Lady Craven, with the image of her daughter in Lord Nicholas's clutches uppermost in her thoughts, was less certain. 'There's no knowing what may be happening,' she kept saying anxiously. 'He is not to be trusted.'

'Yes, he is. Stop fussing, Sophia. Charlotte's not the sort of girl he'd play fast and loose with. There's no shortage of the other kind, if he has a mind to that sort of thing. Heaven knows how many women he's bedded. What's the matter with *you*, Snettisham?'

Her companion had pressed her hand to her mouth. 'Just a little faintness, your ladyship. It will pass.'

'It will have to. We shall not be stopping until nightfall. We can stay at the King's Arms. It is quite tolerable.'

Daylight turned gradually to dusk and they were crossing a lonely section of heathland when the coach shuddered to a sudden, grinding halt. Shouts and curses could be heard outside. Lady Fairfax sighed. 'A highway robber, no doubt. Take off all your jewels quickly, Sophia, and give them to Snettisham to sit on.'

Lady Craven obeyed with trembling fingers and Miss Snettisham, receiving the necklace, bracelet and rings, thrust them beneath her sombre skirts and shrank back between the two ladies to the point of invisibility. Lady Craven clutched at her bare throat. 'What will become of us, Augusta?'

'Nothing,' was the calm response. 'I shall deal with him.'

The door was wrenched open. A masked face thrust itself forward, a pistol was brandished and the stench of the unwashed assailed their nostrils. 'Your money and your jewels or your lives, ladies.'

'We have none, my good man,' Lady Fairfax said coldly, holding a lace-edged kerchief to her nose. 'We have more sense than to travel with either.'

The pistol was waved about again; the rough voice sneered. 'You expect me to believe that? Rich folk like yourselves with no jewels?'

'I am wearing none. Nor is this lady beside me. We have been robbed by the likes of you far too many times. See for yourself.'

A lantern was held aloft as the highwayman saw for himself. It probed further and caught Miss Snettisham in its light, transfixed like a terrified rabbit. 'What about *her*?'

'*Her*?' Lady Fairfax's tone was incredulous. 'She is my paid companion. Of no consequence whatever. She has nothing. However, it is possible that my coachman may have a few coins about him. Kindly close the door and he will give them to you before we proceed on our way.'

Lady Craven held her breath as the man hesitated. Then, to her astonishment, he gave a grunt and slammed the coach door. Within a moment they were once more on the move. Miss Snettisham, with some awkward shifting about, extracted the jewellery from its hiding place and returned it. Sophia Craven reclasped her necklace with hands that still shook. 'Do you really travel without any jewels, Augusta? I can scarcely believe it of you? You are never normally to be seen without a great deal of adornment.'

'Snettisham always conceals anything of value about her person,' Lady Fairfax replied. 'It is all perfectly safe. Nobody would ever think of looking there.'

An hour later they arrived at the King's Arms. Lady Fairfax summoned the landlord. 'Has my nephew been here, Dobson?'

He demurred. 'I'm not certain of that, milady.'

'Stuff and nonsense. You know quite well. Has he, or has he not?'

'Possibly, milady.'

'Possibly?'

'He might have been the night before last.'

'With a party? Another gentleman and two young ladies?'

'I could not say for certain, your ladyship.'

'Nor could you say for certain that he had not been?'

'No, milady.'

Lady Fairfax nodded in approval. 'Ever the soul of discretion, Dobson. Highly commendable in a man of your trade.'

The landlord smiled. 'Your ladyship might be interested to know that a Mr and Mrs

Beauclerc stayed here last night. They were also enquiring after his lordship. Most urgently.'

'Were they indeed? And did you tell them anything?'

'No, milady. But they left in a great hurry very early this morning – in a westerly direction.'

Lady Craven wrung her hands. 'We cannot possibly reach Maplethorpe before them. Mrs Beauclerc will make a most terrible fuss and Charlotte will be embroiled in the scandal. It will be all over London. Everything is lost, Augusta.'

'No, it isn't. Don't be so feeble, Sophia. Where are the salts, Snettisham? Give her a good dose.'

'We must leave at first light,' Lady Craven declared after several deep sniffs.

'I told you that there is no need to gallop after them. We shall arrive at Maplethorpe all in good time and all will be well.'

'So you keep saying, Augusta. But it is not *your* daughter that is in this unfortunate predicament.'

'*Fortunate*, not unfortunate, Sophia. You will thank me, in the end.'

★ ★ ★

'Tell Perkins to go faster, Edwin.'

'I've told him twice, Maria.'

'It will not do. We shall never reach Maple-thorpe in time at this rate.'

The earl jabbed upwards with his stick on the coach roof and the coachman, mistaking his master's wishes, slowed the horses to a trotting pace. The countess lowered the window to lean out. *'Faster,* not slower, you fool.'

'Have a care for the horses,' her husband protested. 'One of 'em could burst a blood vessel.'

'What does that matter? Think of what is at stake, Edwin. Do you want Maplethorpe to go to your brother?'

He shrugged. 'Don't know that I'd mind so much. Damned inconvenient place, if you ask me. Too many rooms.'

'That can very easily be remedied. It is merely a question of removing some of them.'

'Too many draughts as well. And all those infernal passages.'

'There are a great many improvements necessary,' the countess acknowledged. 'The whole house must be *drastically* altered. I have already decided exactly what is required to make it fit to live in.'

'It'll cost money.'

'If Maplethorpe is to be yours, then your aunt will surely also provide you with the means for its improvement and upkeep. After your brother's latest disgraceful and irresponsible behaviour she will be bound to cut him off without so much as a penny.'

'Don't count your chickens, Maria. She's very fond of Nicholas. Told you so before. Always has been.'

'But he has gone too far this time.'

Her husband grunted. 'Nothing new in that.'

After several more miles, the coach gradually slowed to a halt. The earl stuck his head out of the window. 'What's going on, Perkins?'

'One of the horses has gone lame, my lord.'

The countess put her head out of the window on the other side. 'Carry on, at once, Perkins.'

'Can't do that, Maria,' remonstrated her husband, whose finer feelings were reserved for his dogs and his horses. 'Not right at all. What's to do, Perkins?'

'There's an inn just ahead, my lord. The King's Arms.'

'Pull in there then. Getting dark, in any case. We'll stay the night. Change horses. I've had enough of this damn coach.'

The earl remained stone deaf to the countess's protests. He could be a stubborn man, when he chose, and, besides concern for his horse, consideration for his empty stomach overrode all else. The countess gave in with bad grace and, on arrival at the inn, consoled herself by complaining irritably about the landlord's unhelpfulness.

'I asked him if your brother had stopped here recently and he denied it completely.'

'Well, he probably didn't.'

'I think the man was lying.'

'Why should he do that?'

'Nicholas paid him to keep his mouth shut, no doubt. Offer him more, Edwin.'

'Can't very well do that when I don't know how much Nicholas paid the fellow, can I?'

However, when they retired for the night after a meal that had more than satisfied his lordship's hopeful expectations, it transpired that the chambermaid – on receipt of several coins – was able to confirm the countess's suspicions that Lord Nicholas had indeed stayed at the inn two nights before.

'What did I tell you, Edwin?' she said

triumphantly.

'Begging your pardon, milady...' The chambermaid was hovering by the door. 'But there's something else you might like to know.'

'Edwin!'

The earl tossed over another coin.

'A Mr and Mrs Beauclerc were staying here last night, milady. They were asking about Lord Nicholas, too. And they wanted to know if he was alone.'

'Well, *was* he?'

'I couldn't say, milady...'

'Edwin!'

Another coin spun through the air.

'There were two young ladies with him and a military gentleman.

'And did you tell Mr and Mrs Beauclerc this?'

'Yes, milady.

'Did you hear that, Edwin? Miss Beaclerc's parents, undoubtedly, and in full pursuit. We need not worry. They will soon put a stop to things.'

'You mean to their daughter wedding that captain fellow? *If* they get there in time. That's only half the problem, though, ain't it? What about Nicholas and Miss Craven?'

The chambermaid who was still hovering, coughed. 'Begging your pardon, sir...' The earl, unprompted this time, threw another coin. 'Lady Fairfax is staying the night here, too. And Lady Craven with her.'

The countess frowned. 'Your aunt and Miss Craven's mother here in this very inn? That can only mean one thing. They are on their way to Maplethorpe as well. But with what intention exactly?'

The earl had had enough of the whole affair. 'How should I know? Damned stupid goose-chase, if you ask me. Galloping across the countryside, ruining perfectly good horses.'

The countess ignored him, airing her thoughts aloud. 'If Lady Craven is accompanying Lady Fairfax then their journey must be out of concern for Miss Craven and *her* reputation, rather than for Miss Beauclerc or any scandal attaching to Maplethorpe. Which means that your aunt and Lady Craven will be intent on enforcing a marriage between your brother and Miss Craven.' She rounded on her husband. 'We must leave at dawn, Edwin. At very first light. At all costs we must be there before them.'

Seventeen

On the following morning, Amelia and Captain Young walked in the rose garden at Maplethorpe. He was greatly concerned. 'Dear Miss Beauclerc, I hope so much that the unfortunate situation in which we find ourselves has not made you regret the step taken?'

She shook her head. 'Not for one second. My only fear is that Mama and Papa may arrive before we can be married.'

'The parson is on his way,' he assured her. 'And is expected to be here before nightfall. We could be married before the day is out – if that is what you still want?'

'Of course it is! I want it more than anything else in the world.'

'I shall do everything in my power to make you happy, I swear it.'

'I am already happy,' she said simply. 'The happiest person alive. And I wish so much that my dear friend, Charlotte, could be happy too. I had hoped at one time that she might marry Lord Nicholas but I'm afraid it is not to be. She would never accept him now. Not since she learned the truth.'

'The truth?'

'That he only proposed to her so that his aunt, Lady Fairfax, would not disinherit him. I believe she thought that Charlotte could reform him, though I am not sure that *anyone* could do that.'

'How did Miss Craven find this out?'

'Lord Nicholas's sister-in-law told her. The countess is not at all a nice person, you know, but Charlotte believed her to be speaking the truth. So, of course, when Lord Nicholas proposed marriage she refused him.' Amelia paused. 'It *is* true, isn't it? You are such a good friend of Lord Nicholas that I think you must have known about it.'

He said ruefully, 'I am afraid that I *did* know. Like yourself, I had hoped that good might come of it. That if Nicholas and Miss Craven were married they would turn out to suit each other very well.'

'So did I,' she agreed. 'But I suppose that's an end to it. It will never happen now.'

★ ★ ★

Captain Young found his friend out by the kennels, with Marmaduke sitting obediently at a distance while the gun dogs barked through the kennel bars. He drew him aside, wasting no time in preamble. 'Miss Craven knew very well why you proposed to her, Nicholas. Your sister-in-law learned of it by chance and lost no time in informing her. Amelia has just told me.'

He nodded. 'I suspected that she knew, though I could not see how she could have discovered it. Once it came to Maria's ears, by whatever route, she would have lost no time in making mischievous use of her knowledge.'

'I am sorry, Nicholas. Will you really lose Maplethorpe?'

'Undoubtedly. My aunt is a woman of her word.'

'It seems a great pity ... and Miss Craven is altogether admirable.'

'Yes,' Lord Nicholas smiled. 'I admire her very much. Unfortunately, though, she does not feel quite the same admiration for me.' He clapped Captain Young on the shoulder. 'There's no cause for gloom, though, Clive. The parson will be here before long and you and Miss Beauclerc will

242

be safely married and will live happily ever after.'

'I hope you will not think it impertinent of me, Miss Craven, but there is something that I should like to speak of with you.'

'What is that, Captain Young?'

'I believe that you know all about Lady Fairfax's plan for a match between yourself and Lord Nicholas.'

'*Plot* would be a better word.'

'Perhaps so,' he acknowledged. 'And you have every right to feel incensed. But I should like you to know that Nicholas most sincerely admires you – he has told me so himself.'

'Has he, indeed? And did he ask you to tell me?'

'No, he did not. Nor would he. I have been a friend of his for many years and please believe me when I say that there is a great deal of good about him. A very great deal.'

'Lady Fairfax has already tried to convince me of the same thing, and so have you. I found it rather difficult to credit.'

'Nonetheless, it is true. He has many excellent qualities.'

'Lady Fairfax listed all those she could

think of. It was quite a short list.'

He smiled wryly. 'I can see you are determined not to think well of him, Miss Craven. I am sorry for that. Please forgive me for my impertinence. It was well meant.'

Charlotte walked alone for a time in the gardens, trying to collect her thoughts. Captain Young's plea for Lord Nicholas had affected her more than she had allowed him to see. That so upright and honourable a gentleman could think so well of his friend could not fail to impress. *Nicholas most sincerely admires you – he has told me so himself.* Could that really be true? Or was it just another clever ruse? How could she be certain of anything? She walked on down a long alleyway between tall walls of box hedging, reaching high above her head on each side. At the far end she discovered a curved seat, set within an arbour of rambling roses, with a charming marble statue behind of a hoofed Pan playing his pipes. She admired the view for a while – the long, straight vista of clipped hedging, the warm and golden stone of the old house beyond, the sheltering trees and hills surrounding it all in its own peaceful world. It would certainly be a great pity if Maplethorpe were to fall into the hands of the dreadful countess. The more she saw of the place, the more she appreciated its worth and its beauty. And the more she understood why Lord Nicholas should wish so very much to keep it out of the countess's grasp.

In her reverie she did not notice Marmaduke approaching until he was in right front of her, thrusting his head on to her lap. She stroked him and looked up to see Lord Nicholas drawing near. Fortunately, she thought, he could have no inkling of what had been passing through her mind. He asked her permission to sit down beside her.

'This has always been a favourite place of mine,' he remarked pleasantly. 'When I was a child and staying with my aunt, I used to come here on my own.'

He had been motherless from an early age, she reminded herself. A solitary child. Lonely, perhaps, with only his considerably older brother Edwin, for company, who, by all accounts, was dullness itself. 'It's certainly very peaceful.'

'I am sorry that we did not see more of each other in those days,' he went on. 'Or that what little you saw of me was so unpleasant. I must have been altogether odious to have created such a poor impression.'

'You were not so very bad,' she said, anxious to be fair.

'Not so very bad? That is something, at least.' He smiled. 'But not good enough for you to bring yourself to marry me? I don't blame you, Lottie, since you knew all about my aunt's machinations and my own perfidy. No wonder you refused me with such alacrity.'

She coloured, wondering how he had discovered that she knew. From Captain Young, most probably. Well, it scarcely mattered now. 'Your motive hardly recommended you to me.'

'You must have hated me for it.'

'Hate is a very strong word.'

'Despised, then? Detested? Deplored?'

In spite of herself, she smiled. 'Some of all three, I think.'

He went on quietly. 'You have every right to harbour such feelings towards me and I hope that, with time, they may fade. But I still believe, in spite of everything, Lottie, that we should do rather well together.'

'How could we possibly? We do not love

each other.'

'Indeed, we don't – as you rightly remarked to me before. We are already agreed on
that. But our situation is a very practical
start to any marriage, as I pointed out then.
No great expectations. No high hopes. A
mutual understanding. And now it is even
more the case. You know my motive perfectly
– to keep Maplethorpe – and therefore there
can be no longer be any shred of deception
between us. Can there?'

She met his eyes and looked away. 'I
suppose not.'

'And so, I am asking you, once again, to be
my wife.'

She hesitated. Marmaduke thrust his head
once more on to her lap and wagged his tail.
She pushed him away gently and looked at
the old house, so tranquil before her. 'If I
refuse will Lady Fairfax certainly leave
Maplethorpe to your brother?'

'You know enough of her to appreciate that
she is more than capable of carrying out
such a threat.'

'It would be a great pity if your sister-in-
law were to change everything here...'

'It would indeed,' he said gravely. 'Perhaps
you could bring yourself to marry me for the

sake of Maplethorpe? And to save the west wing? A very worthy cause, don't you think? Consider how close you would be living to your old home, Lottie, and to your dear parents. You would be able to visit them frequently and to have them visit here – as much as you liked.' He paused. 'And, of course, it would give them much pleasure to have their grandchildren so near. Who knows, we might even be able to persuade Captain and Mrs Young to take a house close by, too. Not forgetting that Marmaduke and I have become very good friends and he would be more than happy to share us both. All in all, much good could come of it, don't you agree?'

She coloured at the mention of grand-children. But there was a great deal of truth in what he said. Her parents would certainly be as delighted to have her living there, as she would be to be so near them, with Marmaduke to make things perfect. And if Amelia and Captain Young were at hand too ... It would make for a very pleasant arrange-ment all round, the more that she thought about it. And he was quite right that, since she and he did not love each other, there could never be any of the sad disappointment that seemed to bedevil many marriages. It would be strictly a question of convenience – and of saving Maplethorpe. Besides all that, of course, there was no denying that Lord Nicholas could be very agreeable company indeed, when he chose. She did not permit herself to dwell on another attribute, extolled with such frankness by Lady Fairfax.

'Charlotte?' His eyes were fixed on her face. Marmaduke nudged her with his nose.

'Very well,' she said at long last. 'I agree.'

He took her hand in his and kissed it before he drew her to her feet. He smiled down at her. 'Then why waste any more time? Let us make it a double wedding.'

Eighteen

Mr and Mrs Beauclerc had been obliged to spend a further night at another inn, greatly inferior to the King's Arms, while the damage done to their coach was repaired. And not only their conveyance had suffered. Mr Beauclerc had also sustained a number of bruises due to Mrs Beauclerc having fallen on top of him as the coach had overturned. Mrs Beauclerc, her fall broken by her husband, had emerged shocked but unscathed. One wheel of the coach had been broken and there had been no question of continuing their journey. Help was sent for from the nearest town and the Beauclercs passed the remainder of the day and the next night at the Black Bear, which proved to be both uncomfortable and unclean. By the time they were able to set forth on the following morning, Mrs Beauclerc's mood was as black as the bear painted on the inn sign. Several times she thrust her bonneted head out of the window and shouted to the coachman to go faster still. With the horses well rested and refreshed they made a good pace but Mr Beauclerc, nursing his bruises in the corner, groaned as he was tossed this way and that.

'For God's sake, Dorothea! You'll have us in the ditch again.'

'It's life or death!' she declared.

'Life or death? It's about marriage,' he said, adding sourly to himself, 'though, some might call *that* a living death.'

'Do you wish your daughter to be married to a no-good fortune hunter?'

'We don't know that he's no-good. I've never even spoken to the fellow.'

'Well, *I* have. You will allow me to be a very astute judge of character.'

He grunted. 'I didn't think much of some of those others you were so keen on for Amelia.'

'They were all extremely eligible young gentlemen. Any one of them would have made a most suitable husband and son-in-law. Captain Young is a penniless nobody.' Mrs Beauclerc stuck her head out of the window again and gave a gasp of horror.

'There is another coach just ahead. Whose can it be?'

'We are not the only travellers in England,' he told her bitingly. 'Others are permitted to use the highway.'

She took no notice of him, shrieking up to the coachman to overtake at once. As the coach lurched forward she was propelled backward heavily, once again, on to her husband, inflicting yet more bruises.

'I do believe that was the Beauclerc coach that has just passed us, Edwin.' The countess craned her neck to see the back of the conveyance that had galloped by at breakneck speed and was disappearing into the distance. 'I am quite sure I caught a glimpse of Mrs Beauclerc as it went by – no one could mistake her.'

'Or miss her either,' the earl remarked. 'Fattest woman I've ever laid eyes on.'

The countess clutched at his arm. 'They will arrive before us. That must not be.'

'Why not? They'll want to put a stop to their daughter weddin' that fellow she's run off with. They won't care a fig about Nicholas and Miss Craven. Nothing to do with 'em.'

'I do not trust Mrs Beauclerc. She will do only whatever suits her own purposes – unpleasant creature that she is,' the countess said, disregarding her own propensity to do exactly the same. 'Thank goodness Lady Fairfax and Lady Craven, at least, are far behind us.'

'How do you know that? Could be far ahead, for all we know. Might have left long before us.' The earl fanned the flames of his wife's fears. 'Probably get there long before any of us. My aunt has got some damned fine horses. Always known how to pick 'em.'

The countess tightened her thin lips. 'Tell Perkins to go faster, Edwin. We must overtake Mr and Mrs Beauclerc and Lady Fairfax, too, if she *is* ahead. It is vital that we arrive at Maplethorpe before them all.'

'It would seem that my nephew and his wife were also staying here last night,' Lady Fairfax informed Lady Craven casually as they were settling themselves in the coach, preparing to depart from the King's Arms. 'Dobson told me that they left at first light on their way to Maplethorpe – in a *great* hurry, he said. I wonder what mischief Maria is up to.'

Lady Craven looked alarmed. 'Nothing pleasant, I am quite certain, Augusta. I cannot help it, but I do not greatly care for your niece.'

'Nor do I, as it happens, but she and Edwin seem to do well enough together.'

'But why should they be going to Maplethorpe?'

'They have probably learned about Miss Beauclerc's elopement with Captain Young, Nicholas's part in it and Charlotte's involvement in the affair.'

'How could they? I have barely learned of it myself.'

'My dear Sophia, gossip of that kind travels a great deal faster than these horses. It is quite useless to hope that it can be kept a secret.'

'Oh dear, oh dear! Charlotte will be disgraced and die an old maid since nobody will wish to marry her.'

'You forget that Nicholas wants to,' Lady Fairfax reminded her tartly. 'And that is why we are making this journey at this early hour. We are going to make very sure that he does.'

'But if Mr and Mrs Beauclerc should reach Maplethorpe before us, they may ruin everything. Who is to say what kind of trouble and upset *she* might cause?'

'Hmmm. There's some truth in that. Snettisham, tell Barnes to hurry up. I wish to reach Maplethorpe in the fastest possible time. If any other coach stands in our way then he is to overtake it.'

'Dearly beloved, we are gathered together in the sight of God, and in the face of this congregation, to join together this man and this woman – and this man and this woman – in holy matrimony...' The Reverend Aloysius Trimble, mud-caked riding boots showing beneath his hastily donned cassock and surplice, began the marriage ceremony in the candle-lit chapel. To his dismay, not just one couple, but two stood before him at the chapel altar – neither having arrived there by the customary route of banns, familial consent, or anything else that normally preceded a marriage. But on the insistence of Lord Nicholas, whom he well knew to be next in line to the estate – and given his present patroness's advanced years – he had felt it incumbent on him to do as he was told without question or argument. The congregation was made up of a handful of household servants, of which four were to act as witnesses: the butler, two footmen, the housekeeper and the cook. It was all most irregular.

He continued bravely. '...which is an honourable estate, instituted of God in the time of Man's innocency, signifying unto us the mystical union that is betwixt Christ and his Church and therefore is not by any to be enterprised lightly or wantonly to satisfy Man's carnal lusts or appetites...'

The military gentleman, Captain Young, and his bride, standing before him on one side, showed every sign of mutual affection but the same could not be said of the other couple. While Lord Nicholas's eyes were upon his bride, she was keeping *her* eyes fixed firmly upon the flagstones at her feet. The parson sincerely hoped that it was bridal modesty that kept them there, and not reluctance. He had learned enough of his future patron to know that he was capable of all kinds of wild behaviour, which might well include coercing the girl to marry him. He cleared his throat and went on.

'Which holy estate Christ adorned and beautified with his presence, and first miracle that he wrought, in Cana of Galilee...'

★ ★ ★

After following in pursuit of the Beauclercs for some miles, the Earl and Countess of Strickland's coach finally succeeded in overtaking them on a straight stretch of the highway where there was room enough to pass. Mrs Beauclerc had a clear view of the countess's triumphant expression as she went by, while the countess was gratified to see what consternation and fury had been caused in the process. Mrs Beauclerc, naturally, exhorted their coachman to regain their place ahead but the highway had become much narrower, with many twists and turns, and there was no space for such a difficult manoeuvre. It was not until they had passed, one close behind the other, though the pillared gateway into the Maplethorpe estate and gained the long carriageway down to the house that such an opportunity presented itself. Since the way was bordered on each side by firm, flat grass the Beauclercs' coachman, cracking his whip once more, was able to draw alongside the leading conveyance. The two coaches rattled downhill towards the house with both teams of horses galloping neck-and-neck and the two ladies glaring at each other from their respective windows. Not far behind them, a third coach had entered through the gateway and was making ground fast, but those ahead were all too preoccupied with the race to notice.

Mr Trimble cleared his throat again and at some length, as if to emphasize the gravity of the next part of the service. 'I require and charge you both – you both – as ye will answer at the dreadful day of judgement...' How awkward it was with *two* couples, he thought. He was obliged to keep turning his head from one to the other, like a marionette pulled by strings. '... when the secrets of all hearts shall be disclosed, that if either of you – or either of *you* – know any impediment why ye may not be lawfully joined together in matrimony, ye do now confess it. For be ye well assured—'

Even as he had been speaking, the chapel door had crashed open and a very large woman, dressed entirely in purple, burst in. 'Stop the ceremony! Stop it at once, I say! It shall not continue.' She advanced towards the altar, brandishing a furled parasol like a sword and followed by a gentleman considerably thinner and smaller than she. 'Amelia! You shall not marry this man!'

Mr Trimble, shocked by such behaviour,

found his voice. 'This is God's house, madam. I beg you to remember that.'

She gave him a withering look. 'This marriage is against the law. We have not given our consent to it. You must stop the ceremony at once.'

'Continue,' Lord Nicholas commanded him in a steely voice.

He shook his head. 'I fear I cannot, my lord. An impediment has been declared.'

To his further dismay there was more commotion at the chapel door and another lady and gentleman entered in a great flurry. He recognized them immediately as the Earl and Countess of Strickland. The countess paused to take in the scene at a glance and held up her hand. 'Mr Trimble, this must stop. Immediately!'

'I have already told him that,' Mrs Beauclerc informed her icily. 'Though what business it is of yours, I do not know. My daughter is scarcely your concern.'

'Your daughter may marry whomsoever she chooses, for all I care,' the countess retorted. 'It is the *other* couple who must not wed.'

'What other couple?' said Mrs Beauclerc, who in her excitement had quite failed to notice them.

'My brother-in-law and Miss Craven. Lord Nicholas has deceived her. Tricked her into this marriage. *Forced* her into it, for all we know.' The countess stepped forward. 'Miss Craven, we have come to save you from a union that could bring you nothing but misery and humiliation.'

'That is exceedingly noble of you, Maria,' Lord Nicholas remarked smoothly. 'But, fortunately, you are quite mistaken. Miss Craven is marrying me entirely of her own free will. There is nothing to save her from. And so, if you will be good enough to sit down and remain quiet, we shall continue with the ceremony.'

Mrs Beauclerc confronted him. 'Not so fast! Nothing continues without our consent. We will not permit our dear daughter to wed this person of no consequence.'

'Of no consequence, madam?' Lord Nicholas enquired in silky tones. 'Captain Young, a hero of His Majesty's Dragoon Guards? Awarded two of the highest medals for bravery? But perhaps you are not aware of that?'

'I am.' Most unexpectedly, the earl spoke up. 'Just realized who the fellow is. He's the one who helped us finish off Bony at Leipzig. Took on a whole lot of Frenchies single handed. Talk of London.'

'It is of no interest to me who he is, or what he did,' his wife responded sharply. 'It is poor Miss Craven who is my concern.'

Mr Beauclerc, diverted from a painful consideration of his bruises, bestirred himself. 'It's of interest to *me*. I remember now. I knew the name rang a bell. Battle of the Nations. I read all about him in the *Gazette*.'

The earl, who, next to prowess on the hunting field, admired prowess on that of battle, concurred. 'Exactly so, sir. The very gentleman. Damned fine soldier. None braver or better.'

'That should suit you, Dorothea,' Mr Beauclerc said drily. 'Captain Young's far more worthy than all the others put together. I give my consent.'

Mrs Beauclerc paused for a moment's sober reflection. Perhaps she had been rather too hasty in her judgement of the captain. Images of his potential future passed rapidly through her mind's eye – other battles, more medals, consequent promotion – to major, to colonel, to brigadier, to general, to field marshal, even. There was no knowing what might happen in these uncertain times. The French, as everyone knew, were always causing trouble. Precedents flitted before her. A title, certainly, to go with it all. Estates, a grand house – Blenheim Palace and the Duke of Marlborough appeared and went. A glory – ten times greater than anything that some minor scion of an obscure family, titled or no, could confer – might, in the end, reflect upon herself and Mr Beauclerc. 'Perhaps I have misjudged the matter somewhat,' she conceded finally, squeezing herself into a pew and sitting down. 'The ceremony may continue.'

'*Yours* may, Mrs Beauclerc,' the countess told her sharply. 'But the other may not. Miss Craven does not wish it.'

A voice rang out from the chapel doorway and they all turned, as one, towards it. 'As to that, Maria, let us hear what Charlotte has to say. She can speak for herself.' Lady Fairfax stood there majestically, one hand on her ebony stick. Lady Craven was close behind her, while Miss Snettisham hovered in the background. 'Well, Charlotte, do you or do you not wish to marry my nephew – disgraceful and unworthy though he may be?'

There was a moment's silence before the

answer was given, clear enough for all to hear. 'I have agreed to marry him.'

'Of your own free will?'

'Of my own free will.'

Lady Fairfax nodded. 'That is settled, then. And Lady Craven gives her full permission. Is that not so, Sophia?'

'If Charlotte truly consents...'

'She has just declared herself to do so.' Lady Fairfax advanced regally into the chapel, followed by Lady Craven and, at a respectful distance, Miss Snettisham. The first two ladies took seats in the front pew while Miss Snettisham found a place further back. Augusta Fairfax rapped her stick loudly on the flagstones. 'You may proceed, Mr Trimble. And make it as quick as you can.'

'I am well aware of your very natural reluctance to share a bed with me, Lottie. Would you prefer it if I spent tonight in the adjoining room?'

She could not quite credit his consideration; there was something so unlikely about it. So disarming. So confusing. 'It would be best,' she agreed with some relief.

'On the other hand,' he continued, opening

the door and then pausing, as though a casual afterthought had occurred to him. 'We should not overlook the matter of grandchildren – to please your parents. Should we? No doubt they will expect several.'

She swallowed. 'At some point perhaps...'

'We must not, after all, think only and selfishly of ourselves. That would be quite wrong. Don't you think?' He shut the door again. 'Nor must we forget the vital importance of a son and heir to deter all present and future predatory countesses from ever getting their hands on Maplethorpe. I am sure that you agree?'

He was teasing her – she saw that plainly now. Of course, he had had no intention of being so considerate. How could she have imagined that he would? She answered stiffly. 'In the course of time.'

He took her hands and drew her towards him. The kiss, which started quite mildly, went on for some while. Eventually, he said, close to her ear. 'The only trouble, Lottie, is that if we are to achieve all this, there is scarcely a moment to lose.'

Nineteen

True to her word, Lady Fairfax moved into the Dower House, a short distance away from Maplethorpe, the very next day. She had ordered the necessary arrangements to be made several months previously and was able to depart with the minimum of fuss and inconvenience. Lady Craven was prevailed upon to spend a few days there before returning home.

'So you see, Sophia,' Lady Fairfax told her friend, 'I never had the least doubt that my plan would succeed in the end. I always thought that they would be ideally suited to one another.'

'I trust that you will be proved right.'

'Of course I am right. Nicholas has lost his heart to Charlotte. Completely. I have never seen him look at any woman in the way that he looks at her. Haven't you noticed?'

'That may be so,' Sophia Craven acknowledged, who had remarked the very same thing with a fluttering heart. 'But what of poor Charlotte?'

'You're sounding just like Maria. What of her?'

'Well, I have not seen Charlotte look at *him* in anything like the same manner. At the marriage ceremony she did not look at him at all. She does not appear to be in the least in love.'

Augusta Fairfax smiled a slow, cat-like smile. 'My dear Sophia. If she is not yet, she very soon will be. I can promise you that. You may rely on Nicholas. He knows everything there is to know about pleasing a woman.'

There was a faint, strangled sound from the corner. Her ladyship turned round irritably. 'Is something the matter, Snettisham? Are you ill again?'

'Just a slight soreness to the throat, Lady Fairfax.'

'Well you had better sit further away. We certainly do not wish to be infected.'

Miss Snettisham gathered up her needlework and moved to a chair in the far corner of the room. She resettled herself and picked up her needle once more. Her life stretched ahead like one long piece of embroidery. It seemed that was to be her fate – to sit in corners and ply her needle, to listen as others talked, to stay forever an onlooker while others lived their lives. She might as well resign herself to it and forget her dreams. She gave a deep, but soundless, sigh and bent her head over her work again.